Panic Attacks in
PISTACHIO

A Psychological
Detective Story

HENRY ABRAMOVITCH

www.ChironPublications.com

Interior and cover design by Danijela Mijailovic
Printed primarily in the United States of America.

ISBN 978-1-68503-165-7 paperback
ISBN 978-1-68503-166-4 hardcover
ISBN 978-1-68503-167-1 electronic
ISBN 978-1-68503-168-8 limited edition paperback

Library of Congress Cataloging-in-Publication Data

Names: Abramovitch, Henry, 1950- author.
Title: Panic attacks in pistachio : a psychological detective story / Henry Abramovitch.
Description: Asheville, NC : Chiron Publications, [2023] | Summary: "Panic Attacks in Pistachio: A Psychological Detective Story begins in the middle of a panic attack and never lets up. The man suffering from these agonizing panic attacks comes to his regular therapy session but instead of finding comfort discovers something no patient would ever expect to find. The drive to discover the truth behind this terrifying mystery sets him out on a quest, even a crusade, to discover the meaning of what happened. He must search among his fellow patients and ultimately enter his therapist's temenos, the holy of holies. In this psychological detective journey, he finds powerful help, through active imagination, from the greatest detectives of all time, Sherlock Holmes and Hercule Poirot. These inner figures help him solve the mystery and the process helps transform tragedy into the beginning of individuation. He discovers many secrets and ultimately the hidden connection between pistachio ice cream and his panic attacks. Written as a thriller, told in the first person, based on the author's long experience as a Jungian analyst, the book makes compelling reading"-- Provided by publisher.
Identifiers: LCCN 2023026732 (print) | LCCN 2023026733 (ebook) | ISBN 9781685031657 (paperback) | ISBN 9781685031664 (hardcover) | ISBN 9781685031688 (limited edition paperback) | ISBN 9781685031671 (ebook)
Subjects: LCGFT: Psychological fiction. | Thrillers (Fiction) | Novels.
Classification: LCC PR9510.9.A27 P36 2023 (print) | LCC PR9510.9.A27 (ebook) | DDC 823/.92--dc23/eng/20230807
LC record available at https://lccn.loc.gov/2023026732

LC ebook record available at https://lccn.loc.gov/2023026733

Chapter 1

It was happening again.
I had to see her.
I couldn't stand it:
Sweating

Being dizzy
Heart pounding so hard you knew you were going to die
Right now.
Die.
Alone, in the middle of the street, in pain.

Only I had been enough times to the ER to know
it wasn't a heart attack.
Or not a heart attack in the sense of something wrong with
    my heart muscle.
It was a different kind of heart attack
A heart attack in my soul.

I had to see her.
She was the only one who helped.
I had to…

It wasn't anything she said,
It was her presence
mostly her eyes,
how she sat,
the pictures in her room
With her, with them
I felt…
Safe in a way that I had never felt safe before
Like a baby smiling into his mother's eyes:
Her seeing me,
Me seeing her seeing me,
seeing her.
It was like you had been listening to the radio all your life
But you never knew it was always on static staccato
and then…
suddenly somebody touched the knob
and then…
you heard sweet, clear music for the very first time.
That's how I felt.
Like I was safe
for my very first time.
Safe from the outside, in.

But not today.
Today,
the static was turned back on high.
And it wouldn't go away.

I had to see her.

I had this repeating dream.
It was like those dreams when you know you need to run…
from the nameless dread.
But you cannot move;
your feet are stuck in frozen space and you wake

2

… in terror.
That was the feeling in the dream.

Only there was no Monster.
In the dream,
I am 6 years old strolling with my mother in the mall.
We are walking together, holding hands, and she asks me
    casually,
"Would you like some ice cream?"
We walk over to the ice cream counter and she says,
"You can have any flavor you want."
I move closer to the frosted glass and look down at my
choices.
Choosing the right ice cream is a challenge for a six-year-old.
Finally, I lift my head, my decision made
I tell my Mom,
who tells the ice cream man,
"Pistachio."
And then…
I awake up in terror.
Whenever I hear kids say, "Let's go get some ice cream."
I break out into searing, scintillating sweat.

The dream feels like an exercise in theology.
The Fate of an entire universe is dependent upon my choice
    of ice cream.
If I choose the wrong flavor, the cosmos implodes.

Maybe it's something inherent in the color:
Not as bright as lime, nor as drab as olive, or blue as sea foam;
pistachio is a soft, muted shade of green
in the realm of sage, honeydew, warm mint, and light moss.
Pistachio feels refreshing in any form.
Anyway, that's the fashion industry's hype.

Did you know that pistachio nuts are amazingly ancient?
Humans have been crunching them for 9,000 years,
if you believe the archeologists,
and I do.
Veteran trees can live for 450 years; there is one carbon
    dated in Israel.
Most people prefer Persian pistachio but for pure pleasure,
you must go to the small Sicilian village of Bronte—yes like
    the sisters—and there,
you can find…pistachio heaven.
But I am just trying to distract the panic.

I had to get to see her…now!

One of the toughest problems in seeing my therapist was
    parking.
In the movies, no one ever has to look for a space;
there is always one waiting.
Have you noticed?
There are ten thousand books
about therapy and psychoanalysis.
But not one describes the struggle
to find your parking space.
It becomes
the metaphor for looking for your place.
No one sings
the parking space therapy blues, like it is.
Well, maybe, Yalom.
Love's Executioner.
That essay is my favorite.
It shows so well how therapists can really help their patients,
yet have no idea why.

To paraphrase Shakespeare:
Some people are born with an inherent ability to finding
   parking spaces;
others learn to find it;
Those who are "parking blessed" always know where to find
   them.
They learn the rhythms of their therapist's neighborhood.
Others go round and round and feel that
even God has forgotten them.
When I was born,
God had a cold.
Parking was a savvy skill that eluded me.
But.
Today, I was lucky.

Right in front of the office,
where there **never ever** was a place to park;
there was a gap.
It seemed like a sign.
Parking space now, peace of mind later.
So, I thought.
But, boy oh boy! was I wrong!

I walked up the steps,
taking two at a time
and entered the waiting room.
Normally, Dr. Engelman…
She told me to call her, "Batsheva,"
has the door open for me,
welcoming me.
"If the door is open," she says, "then you can come right in.
If the door is shut, wait until the exact time and then knock."
But the door had always been open.
Welcoming. Until now.
Today it was shut.

I looked at my cell phone.
There was three minutes to go.
I was early.
In a minute, she would open it.
I imagined her wonderfully, calming eyes.
I would sit down in the comfy chair and I could breathe.
I could forget my nightmares
and never have to choose ice cream again.
I looked at the door.
I had never really seen it.
It was made of special acoustic foam plastic simulated to
     look like real wood,
Walnut, I think.
Since the door was always open, I never had to deal with
     that horrible existential moment of
knocking and waiting ... being up against
the abyss and salvation.
It was time.
I went to the door.

How do you know how to knock at the entryway to therapy?
Is it knock, knock? Like the joke.
"Knock, knock."
"Whose there?"
"Boo."
"Boo Who?"
"Why are you crying?"
Stupid but true.
Is it a rat-tat-tat rhythm? or a sharp staccato, **tat-tat**?
Or perhaps, a well-tempered beat, like a clavier.
I went for steady rhythm: knock, knock, knock; and waited.
Nothing.
Silence.
I was getting sweaty and panicky.

I know what she would say:
She would say,
"It's your abandonment anxiety popping up again."
And I would say, "That's not funny;
Please never do that again,
leaving me alone outside your door."

Only I would never say that to her out loud,
but think it inside with all my might and all my soul.
I waited
and then knocked again.
Louder.
Still nothing and more nothing.
Should I knock again?
What if she was in there… with a patient?
I put my ear to the door.
I could not hear anything
but that didn't mean much since the door
was so soundproofed.
I didn't know what to do.
I was in unknown territory;
like when your plane is diverted to a strange country from
    which there are no follow-on flights.
I looked at my cell phone.
She was almost 2 minutes late.
My cell phone told me I should try to call her.
But first, I thought, I will send her a text message;
if she didn't answer, then I would call.
I wrote tentatively:
"I thought we had our regular eleven o'clock session today."
I debated whether to add: "Is everything all right?"
I wasn't sure what was the protocol for a missing therapist.
So, I just left it out and pressed: "Send."
I placed myself back in the chair of the waiting room.

I checked the phone three times in next three minutes.
Nothing.
So then, I decided to call.
I called.
Her number rang and rang until the ringer went into her
     "oh so familiar" answering machine voice:
"I am sorry I am not able to take your call, in person,
but if you leave a message,
I will try to get back to you as soon as possible."
Beep.
It was as familiar as the safety instructions before take-off.

I left a message.
The same as the text only this time I added,
"Is everything OK?" Beep.
I didn't know whether
To stay or to leave;
that was the question.

I wondered if she had just forgot our appointment.
Therapists were supposed to be elephants.
They never forget.
Only they do.
Sometimes.
I remember this friend.
Jules.
He came to his appointment at a new time and
he also found the door locked.
He waited
and knocked.
Waited and knocked. Waited and knocked.
Double checked his calendar.
No, it was the right day, the right time
Finally, he knocked again loud,

and was astonished when the therapist opened the door to
    see he was sitting with an elderly woman.
The therapist had forgotten
to make the change in his electronic calendar.
The therapist felt awful.
My friend felt terrible.
The therapist felt awful that the patient felt terrible
at something that was his fault.
My friend felt bad for what he was causing the therapist to feel
so it really was his fault after all.
The elderly woman was waiting,
not understanding.

Finally, the therapist said,
"Let's talk about it at our next session on Thursday."
My friend said "Sure."

Only he never went back.
His Dad had died when he was twelve.
He had been on a camping trip with the Scouts when it
happened and didn't even get back in time for the funeral.
and he could not take another abandonment.
The therapist who was a good guy
kept calling asking him to come in
But he never even picked up.
He didn't want to face the feeling that
it was somehow all his fault.

But for me if she just forgot,
that would be embarrassing,
but such a relief.
Actually.
My fantasies immediately race to the deeper tragedies:
Traffic accident,

fatal illness,
suicide.
That sort of thing.
I debated again:
should I leave or should I stay?
Part of me wanted to stick around and see what happened
when her next client showed up.
But the sliver of the optimist in me said,
"Try knocking one more time. **Hard**."
I walked up to the door, more boldly.
I gave the door two seriously hard knocks. **Rat! Tat!**
And I cried out,
"Dr. Engelman?
Batsheva?
Are you there?"
Nothing
and more nothing.
Total silence. Deeper nothing.
Or was there something?
Something seemed different.
Something seemed changed.
Was it just my imagination?
I looked more closely.
When I had hit the door hard, something **had** moved,
however, miniscule.
The door was no longer firmly flush to the doorframe.
There was a tiny crack, like in the Leonard Cohen song.
What should I do?
I couldn't leave now;
but to enter was
like forcing your way into
the holy of holies of healing.
What Jung called the "Temenos,"
that sacred space at the Center.

It would be spiritual breaking and entering.
Yet, I could not help myself.
I had to see what was happening inside.
I knew
it was just going to be an empty office;
that she left quickly to pick up
her granddaughter and forgot to lock up.
But it wasn't like her.
She had presence.
Memory.
Her Presence was wide as an ocean.
Her Memory as deep as the Sea.
I pushed the door open
And then...

I saw her.

Chapter 2

She was sitting in her chair,
slouched over,
which certainly was not like her.
She always sat upright.
Showing through her posture a noble righteousness
showing that you, too,
could be the person you were meant to be.
Sitting tall. Upright.
Half of my therapy came from just looking at how she sat.
Upright. *Yashar.*
As if to say, "You, too, can be…"
even when you were lying
smashed to pieces on the floor.
I called her name again.
"Dr. Engelman? Batsheva?
Are you all right?
Do you need help?
Do you want me just to leave?"
I did not know what to do.
There is no protocol for finding your therapist lying
    unresponsive in her chair
….*slouching!*

I took a step closer.

I could now see she was not moving...

not breathing.

I rushed forward trying to find a pulse.

But then saw she was **really** not breathing.

I knew I should start mouth to mouth.

I knew that...

But first, I knew I had to check her pupils.

To see if they would dilate.

I snapped out my cell phone and turned on the light and
splashed it on her face.

I had never seen her face so close.

It seemed so... uncanny.

As if time was slowing.

As if there was a flashbulb going off.

I said to myself: "Focus on the pupils.

Were they dilating?

Was there any difference between left and right?"

Her pupils flashed back deep but motionless.

I touched the skin. It was clammy and cold.

I struggled to find a pulse.

Any pulse. Weak or erratic.

Again, nothing and more nothing.

Inside I was panicking. Inside I was screaming no! no! no!

I knew I had to breathe into her.

The thought of putting my lips to hers felt like incest
through and through.

Spiritual, physical, sexual you name it.

There were many things you could do with your therapist
but putting lips to lips was definitely not one of them.

I couldn't do it.

I must.

I just went ahead without thinking and the weirdest things
     going through my head that I don't even want to tell you
     about.
After minutes of huffing and puffing,
I realized there was nothing to do.
She had passed.
I was supposed to save her and I didn't.
I felt guilty all the way down.
Don't worry, as soon as I saw something was not right,
I pressed SOS button on my phone so I knew real help,
professional help, was on the way.
I knelt down and said, "Forgive me!
I didn't know how to save you.
Will I be damned like Cain to wander restless and
homeless?
Please say you forgive me."
But of course, she couldn't.
She was dead and would never speak again.

I stood up and glanced around, looking at her desk where
     she wrote receipts at the end of the month.
There was something there.
A large oversize piece of paper waiting to be read.
Although I was still in the shock of trauma, I walked over
     and saw.
It was a suicide note:
"I, Dr. Batsheva Engelman being of sound mind and body
     have decided that my life is no longer worth living and
     therefore have decided to end it now.
Please do not attempt any efforts to prevent this.
My will is in the drawer by my bed at home.
To my patients, I say farewell.
Perhaps we will meet on the other side."
It was signed Dr. Batsheva Engelman!

Chapter
3

Before I understood, the door smashed open and the
 emergency response team entered.
Seeing Batsheva slouched on the chair, they went to work.
Pulse.
Blood pressure.
Oxygen levels.
Shot directly into the heart.
Mouth to mouth and simultaneously cardiac compressions.
One, two, three; one, two, three.
"Ok. Let's call it. 12:54 p.m."
"Are you the guy who called it in?
Listen, must be tough on you.
But she was dead before you opened that door.
Looking at rigor, body temperature, pallidity…
I'd say she's been dead for couple of hours.
At least, she didn't suffer.
No drooling; no postural changes; no defensive wounds.
We'll only know at autopsy, but I would guess heart.
The old ticker.
The coroner or medical examiner will be on his way.
Are you her relative or something?"
I mumbled, "We had… a special relationship."

"Ok, whatever you say."

I moved so that I was facing the emergency guy with my back
leaning on the table so he would not see the note.

I couldn't let him or the medical examiner/coroner see that
note.

Anyway, it wasn't true. It couldn't be true.

How traumatic can a session be!

To find your therapist dead just when you need her most is
a tragedy.

To discover that she killed herself is a catastrophe that cannot
be contained in words.

Only in howls.

I needed to get him out of the room.

"Excuse me, Sir,

I want to thank you and your team for doing all you could to
save her.

For you it's routine but for me it's a shock.

Can I have just a few minutes alone,

you know, to say my goodbyes?

She was someone…who was so very important to me.

I'm sure you understand."

"I'm not supposed to do it but since it's probably just a ticker
case, I will let you have five minutes alone.

I'll be just outside the door.

Just make sure you don't touch anything or move the body."

"Thank you so much."

He left and I went for the letter immediately.

I read it again.

I couldn't believe it.

I couldn't understand it.

I couldn't.

It was like pistachio ice cream all over again.

No way out. No way in.

I grabbed a bunch of other stuff on the desk and then impulsively

I grabbed another piece of her hand writing, the list of her patients.

I know it sounds like some cheap thriller.

But believe you me, I would prefer any sleuth who could flip this reality into fiction.

I looked at her lying there.

Messed up by the attempts to revive her.

Slouched in a way I never saw her.

Dead in a way I never saw her.

I saw her as "Not Batsheva" and felt what can be only called…, a countertransference from the dead.

I put the papers in my jacket inner pocket

and fled.

Chapter
4

Just as I was rushing out the door,
in came a cop, and a guy in a white coat.
"Stop!"
The cop shouted.
"Are you the Joe that found the body?"
I nodded.
"I thought so.
Listen buddy, you found her, you gotta make a statement
    now and later appear at the inquest.
Everything is criminal
until we know it's not.
Sit down. Hey, relax."
How could I relax when my therapist had just terminated
    herself?
How do I hide that note from this goddamn cop?
I started shaking.
"Oh, I got it," the cop says. "You're a virgin.
First timer.
Never saw someone dead before."

I was shaking even more.
He put his hand on me like a father to his son,

like a father who has seen it all and is initiating his beloved
    son into the horrors of life.
"Do you know what the Stoics used to say?:
'When I am here, death is not; when death is here, I am not."
So what's to be afraid of?
Were you afraid of the time before you were born?
Nobody is.
What comes after death is only more of the same."

It was the opposite of true, but not untrue;
somewhere in the grey zone there was a universe of soggy
    snow
 greying my soul.
I knew what was coming next.
And it came like a cannonball.
"What was your relationship with the deceased?"
"What was my relationship to my savior, my rod, my green
    pasture;
how did she heal me, let me count the ways?"

I tried to mumble my way out. "I knew her for three years."
Of course, he didn't buy.
"Listen buddy.
You think this old farting cop is stupid.
Even cops got computers.
We look 'em up en route.
We know the lady was a professionally qualified Psycho…
So 'fess up.
You were going to her 'cause you thought you were a total
    nutcase, inside of just playing the numbers like a normal
    scumbag."
Now defiantly, even proudly, I said:
"Yes, she was my therapist. And she helped me a lot."
Then bursting into tears, I sobbed:

Chapter 4

"I can't believe….I can't believe….that I will never see her
  again."
"Now, now." he said just like Humphrey Bogart at the end of
  Casablanca.

"Just tell me what happened."

And I did.

Chapter
5

When I finished, he said, "Sign here.
And here.
And here.
You'll have to testify at the inquest.
You'll get a text message.
Saying the when and the where.
Try not to think about."
Try not to think about it!
It's like trying not to think of elephants,
after somebody says, "Don't think about elephants."

Of course, I was going to think about it.
It was the only thing I could think about.
I felt malevolent pleasure that
I withheld her suicide note from my statement.
Let them prove it was ever there.
Let them suspect me of criminal suppression.
But…
let her good name be preserved.
I know I needed to hold onto Batsheva as I knew her:
noble, wise, healing.

Why would she want to take her own life?
Why would she do this to her patients?
To me?

I had to find out.

When I left the building, I came out on the street.
Everything was the same and yet it was all
uncanny.
I blanked out.
I didn't know where I was.

Suddenly, I remembered I had come by car
but had no idea where it was.
I walked up and down the street,
first on one side and then the other.
I remember finding parking here was always hard.
I stopped to gather my head.
I needed a think.
How can I find it?

I remembered hearing there were three rules for finding lost
     objects.
Rule Number 1:
Where did you last see?
Rule Number 2:
Where is supposed to be?
Rule Number 3:
Where can't it be?

Where did I last see my car?
I remembered getting into the car at home.
That was when I last remember seeing it.
But from then it seemed blank.

Where is it supposed to be?
Somewhere in the neighborhood but
as far as possible from where I was standing.
That's where it usually was.

Where couldn't it be?
It couldn't be in front of the office because
there was never, ever a spot there.
And then it hit me like sucker punch.
I was standing in front of the car,
because of this worst of all possible days,
I had the ironic fortune of finding
a space in front of the office.

I opened the door.
Turned the key
and fled.

Chapter
6

Why do therapists kill themselves?
I googled it.
I discovered lots of surprising information.
First of all, it was not uncommon.
Twenty-five percent of therapists admitted to having
suicidal thoughts.
And there were some super famous cases,
like Lawrence Kohlberg,
the Harvard psychologist who wrote the book
on the stages of moral development.
Sad. Ironic. Immoral?
Even old Papa Freud died by "physician assisted suicide."
"Just don't let me suffer," is what he said.

Substance abuse, depression, loss, but especially legal and/
    or ethical investigations were on the royal road to self-
    murder.
Maybe she was under investigation. I could check.
I also discovered that therapists are supposed to have a
    professional will and clinical executor, the poor schmuck
    who had to tell the patients that their beloved healer will
    not be keeping any more appointments.

Some patients felt their therapist's suicide made them ask
    themselves:
How can I believe anything the therapist had said?
It was all sham.
"The patient will disregard everything the therapist said
and his interpretations will be stricken..."
Healer beware thy sting. Be the Wounded healer.
But, not the healer wounding everlasting.

I know I was supposed to be angry at her.
But I wasn't.
Maybe I was still in shock.
But I just didn't get it.
It didn't make sense.
I needed a psychological autopsy.
To find out what was going on in the days before her death.
Was she depressed?
Drugged up?
Ethically compromised?

I realized that if she left that list in the office,
she didn't have a clinical executor
and the letter, pathetic as it was, was her professional will.
I realized I could pretend to be her clinical executor
and call her patients.
Tell them she was dead and trawl them for information.
At the same time, I could use my computer skills to find out
    more about her,
and yes, also about her patients.
Just to be sure, I would take the papers I stole from the
    office to a handwriting expert.
At least he could say for sure whether they were written by
    the hand of the same person.
It was deceitful, I know.

But situational ethics demands improvisation.
And this was a situation.
I had to know what really happened;
working the case could help me not to think about what her
    death meant for me.
I looked up at the ceiling and a haiku popped up in my mind:

In Kyoto,
hearing the cuckoo,
I long for Kyoto.

Chapter
7

I looked at her patient list. Seventeen names with phone numbers.
These were… my brothers-and-sisters in therapy.
We couldn't comfort each other because we were stranger-orphans.
If I passed them on the street, we would never know we had shared a Great Mother.
That we were sitting shiva together, alone.
Just as therapy recreates the status of an only child, so too, in mourning, we were solo survivors.
But for now, grief must wait.
If I was going to pretend to be her clinical executor,
I had to get some pointers.
I googled again.
Here is what I understood.
Be firm,
but empathetic.
Keep it simple.
Speak.
Pause.
Continue.
Repeat.

"Are you Madame X?" Pause.

"I have some bad news."

Longer pause.

"Dr. Batsheva Engelman, your therapist, has died suddenly."

Reflect feeling: "I know this must come as a shock."

Pause. Let it sink in.

"No. We do not know the cause of death yet."

Wait.

"Yes. There will be an inquest.

Dr. Engelman left instructions for me to contact you.

If you are feeling distressed, I could arrange for you to see a bereavement counsellor.

OK. You will let me know."

Empathy.

"I know this must be very hard for you."

Pause.

"Yes."

Pause

"Oh, and one last question, how did she seem at your last session?"

"Just as usual, you say."

"I see.

Here is my telephone number and email

in case you wish to be in touch."

"...Yes.

An enormous loss.

I don't know how we will go on without her."

That was the script.

I had never understood how pretending to be someone else could be satisfying.

But now, for the first time, I understood what a successful actor must feel.

Chapter 7

The first patient I called had seen her at 8 a.m. that very morning.

She said she was as always:

"Warm, sensitive, insightful."

Not exactly what you would think of a woman about to end her existence.

The next person I called didn't answer and it went into answering machine.

Beep.

"Hello.

You have reached the phone of Henri Decavalier, head of the Consular Service of the Republic of France.

You can leave a message after the beep."

Beep.

I said who I was and that to please call me back as soon as possible.

I didn't want him to come to her sealed door and find out that way.

Do people even listen to answering machines anymore?

Maybe if you are a Consul you have to. You might get messages from desperate fellow countrypersons at any hour. So yes, he probably would check his message. Desperate, urgent calls are probably routine for him. He did not grow up with selfies and a vocabulary limited to the false internet intimacies of "like" and "friend."

Maybe he was only an Honorable Consul…

But just then the phone rang. "'Allo. This is Henri Decavalier, French consul. May I speak to…"

"Speaking. Mr. Decavalier, I have bad news. Pause. I believe you are acquainted with Dr. Batsheva Engelman."

"Yeees?"

"I am afraid to say that she died today…suddenly in her office."

"But that cannot be!"

"Yes, I know it must be a shock."

"It is more than a shock. It is a catastrophe."
[pause]
"I can arrange for you to see a bereavement counsellor…"
"At my last session, I gave her something of importance… of
    great personal significance.
Do you think it might be possible for me to enter her office
    in order to retrieve it?"
"You would have to talk to the police. They locked up and
    sealed the room as a possible crime scene. They won't
    know until after an autopsy."
"I see…would it be possible to meet?"
I didn't know what to say. I could fake being a clinical
    executor, but could I carry off being a bereavement
    counsellor?
I remember they once programmed a computer to give
    therapy.
It basically took the end of the patient's sentence and played
    it back to them.

Patient: "I am feeling so sad."
Computer: "Sad?"
Patient: "Yes, I used to rely on her to keep me stable during
    dark times."
Computer: "Dark times?"
Patient: "Yes, sometimes I would wonder whether life was
    worth living."
Computer: "Tell me more."

I know it sounds idiotic but it actually worked pretty well
    until the patients realized it was a computer and not a
    person.
The internet guide for grief counseling said there were a few
    rules of thumb:
"When you don't know what to say, say nothing."

"Use your body language to show empathy."
"Say things like, 'This must be very hard for you.'
Or 'It's so sudden.'"
Maybe I could fake my way through.
I replied to the Consul's query very casually,
"Of course, we can meet."

Chapter 8

The next person on the list just starting moaning,
then weeping and finally whimpering.
After telling her that she could call, I finally hung up the
    phone.
I remembered that I wanted to do the same.
I imagined how she was feeling just now.
Shocked.
Full of Loss.
Numbed.
As though a giant black hole invaded the landscape of her
    existence.
And any moment you might fall in and never come out.
I was frozen.
Frozen outside my grief.
I heard the sounds of grief, but not its music.
Everything slithered in slow motion.
Some inner voice said.
"You should listen to music."
"Verdi? Britten?"
"No!
The Beatles:

'You say goodbye, but I say hello.'"

When the voices came on, I burst into tears.

Chapter 9

I don't know how long I wept. Alone there in the dark.
I only know my shirt was sticky with moisture of my tears.
They say that tears were God's consoling gift to humanity.
Maybe they are right.
I needed:
Her. Her presence. Her eyes, like arms embracing.

I decided to stop calling for today.
Tomorrow was another day.
Maybe I should eat something. Maybe I should sleep.
I went to bed, or rather I was so tired, my bed went into me.
But instead of sleeping, I had long tortuous dreams.
The only scene I remembered clearly was:
I was sitting in a session with Batsheva.
In the dream, I remember asking her
why she was so nice to me
when my ex had been such a total refrigerator.
Then abruptly, I turned to her and said,
"Yes, but you have something important to tell me."
She said, "Yes, I do."
She continued speaking in a matter-of-fact voice:
"I am dead."

But then, she went on looking at me with piercing eyes.
Batsheva's office looked the same as usual,
only it started becoming cold, very cold.
Cold and full of smoke.
and I knew I had to get out fast.
But I couldn't move.
Something cold, smoky and evil was coming closer.
I awoke screaming.

I remember learning in my anthropology seminar
that there were a people who lived in the High Andes,
the Jivaro.
When a family member was murdered,
an avenging soul
was created inside one of the relatives.
This avenging soul would give the person no rest
until vengeance was exacted.

Then I realized.
The funeral!
The funeral would give me perfect opportunities to find out
    more about her and her patients;
I could even try to set up a WhatsApp group for support but
    really to subtly, imperceptibly, seek out information.

Chapter
10

I remember the pages I had stolen from the office. Now I realized I had a way to check to see if the suicide note was false or true. The handwritten list of her patients (which I was using) was certainly hers and I recognized the style from the receipts she wrote out. I ran to get a few from my files. Yes, you could see the loopy "l"; the wobbly "w" and the slanting "c." It was hers for sure. The suicide note looked the same, but I couldn't know for sure. I would need forensic analysis of her handwriting. Maybe it wasn't hard science but it **was** admissible in court, unlike lie detectors which could be so easily faked.

Once again Dr. Google came to the rescue.

There were a dozen experts listed.

How to choose?

What did I know about handwriting and its experts?

I called and made an appointment.

Just after I finished, I got a text message. Someone else **had** created a group of Batsheva's patients, former patients I will have to get used to saying. The text said that Batsheva's funeral was to be tomorrow at 11 a.m. at Shaarei Shamayim Cemetery. I knew I had to go even though it meant facing reality. I was yearning for fantasy. For waking up and seeing it was all a vicious nightmare I would have to tell Batsheva. Would she say I had death wishes toward her, like Freud told Jung en route to America. Maybe that's why Jews bury so quickly so that you have to see death for what it is. Death and nothing else.

The phone rang.

It was Mahdi Jafari. Another one of Batsheva's patients for whom I had left a message to call. I had to remember that I was somebody else for him. He was upset, on the cliff of grieving.

"Yes, it was a shock." I found myself saying. "Yes, I found the body. Yes, it was certain that she was dead."

He too kept saying "I can't believe it. I can't believe it." Then he said something that made my hair have goosebumps. "I left something important in the office. Is there any way, I can retrieve it?"

It was the same thing, virtually word for word that the Consul had said.

What precious thing do you give to your therapist? Some precious *momento*; something you wanted her to protect for you. I couldn't help myself and asked, "Are you by any chance in the diplomatic corps?" He laughed, a real belly laugh.

"Not at all. I'm in transport."

I realised that he didn't even inquire why I had asked.

We said we would meet at the funeral.

Something was going on but I had no idea what it was.

Chapter 11

The next day was the funeral day. It came up heavy with clouds and grief. I knew I had to go, but I felt numb. Robotic. I guess it was shock, or dissociation. I don't know how I got to the funeral home. Waze spoke and I obeyed. Does anybody like funerals? I once knew this guy, some kind of weird anthropologist. He loved going to funerals. Because he said a funeral is "show time." In the face of loss, the culture must show what life is all about, what values it cares about. What makes life worth living in the face of the blue-eyed boy, Mister Death. He was a true participant-observer. He said he had an advantage over many other fieldworkers since no one ever asked him what he was doing there.

At Batsheva's funeral, there were only about 25 people there. Much less than I expected. Maybe it was the weather. Maybe it was the suddenness. Maybe....The service was led by an orthodox Jewish Rabbi, wearing a skull cap. He starting by singing *El Malei Rachamin, Lord full of compassion.* Then he asked forgiveness for Batsheva. Finally, he chanted the Kaddish prayer. *Yitkadol Veyitkadash...*Then to my astonishment, he said there would be no eulogy since it was *Rosh Hodesh*, the First Day of the New Month and it was not custom to give eulogies on such days.

I was taken aback. I felt cheated. I wanted to hear Batsheva's praises raised up toward the Heavenly Throne. What a devoted therapist she was; what a person of *hesed*, loving kindness; that she was the ultimate *mensch*. I expected him to ask the audience if anyone wanted to share some memories. But here too, there was nothing and more nothing. It was as if lips were moving toward lips, romantic music was playing; you already feel the satisfaction of embracing your beloved, only to find yourself alone, falling into darkness descending. I wanted to scream, but it came out only as silence.

The Rabbi then asked for people to step forward to be pallbearers. I knew the right thing was to step forward and do this *true* act of loving kindness: **true** because there was no possibility that Batsheva could ever return the *mitzva*. But I held back. Did I want to be so close to her again? Bearing her weight? Finally, I decided to do the right thing but by then others had stepped up and my hesitation led to my exclusion. As the cortège stepped outside, it started raining. A real cascade. In the movies, rainy funerals are standard, with the heavy symbolism of nature weeping. But in Victorian times, rain at funerals was seen as an indication that the deceased was on their journey toward paradise and a lightning clap the signal that they had arrived. We marched through the muddy ground and saw her lowered in. I noticed the graves of her husband and children next to her. She must have followed the tradition and pre-acquired that grave long ago, to be next to them. Reunited, at last. At least now, she was coming home.

One more Kaddish and we were done. There were no "mourners" so we did not form the two lines for them to pass through. Off to the side, I suddenly noticed the police officer who had taken my statement. If he was here, then they were treating her death as suspicious. Like in B movies, he was here to look over the suspects. Including me.

I started having another panic attack. Sweating. Heart beating. Feeling like I was about to die. It was so familiar yet always felt like the first time. I tried to tell myself that I was not going to die; to take slow deep breathes; to concentrate on being on the seashore, warm in the caring sun. I shut my eyes and pulled myself back from that abyss. When I opened my eyes, the policeman was standing in front of me.

He spoke:

"Death ends life but not the relationship.

I heard she was quite a gal."

"She is…was. She was for me…the best."

"Mmh," he nodded.

"Anyway, the inquest is tomorrow. Here's your subpoena. 2 o'clock."

"Can you tell me anything, autopsy, forensics?" I asked in a pathetic, squeamish voice.

"You'll hear everything tomorrow. Tomorrow."

And he moved away. I saw him giving subpoenas to a few other people. I wondered who they could be. But just then my phone beeped. it was a new WhatsApp group called Batsheva's Bereaved. It was sent out by the Consul. He must have used the new app where you can send messages to anybody near you. He invited everybody who was mourning for Batsheva to come to a "wake" immediately following the end of the funeral at the French Consulate R.S.V.P.

I replied "Coming." It was my chance to meet my sisters and brothers in grief.

I needed to know more about her last days. I got into my car and let Waze lead the way.

At the Consulate, the lines were moody and security was full of intense adjectives: tight, heavy, full.... Everything you owned was sprayed with x-rays. On the floor, the etch-a-sketch lines indicated how to stand while positrons shot through you. And finally, the final pat down. Then I was through. We were hushed into a sober conference room with lights obscured and an oval table with swivel seats. The conference room had room for a full eighteen, but now, there were only nine of us.

Looking at my grieving sisters and brothers, I felt close to these people I had never seen before. Our dress code ranged from to jeans and tie (me) to diplomatic *elegans*. The Consul was in charge. Acting as host, he said we should stand for a moment's silence in memory of *Madame Docteur Batsheva Engelman*. And we did.

When we sat down, he invited each of us to introduce themselves and share a memory of Batsheva. The first one to speak said he was John Cohan, CFO of a Financial Equity Firm. He thanked the Consul for hosting us. "Dr. Engelman," he went on, "was a truly, dignified person who led me through my most difficult times." You could see he wanted to say more but choked down a sob. He looked down.

The woman next to him also had her head down and she waived her turn away with a flabby hand motion. Only then could I hear her gently sobbing. The next person was a very tall and muscular woman. She stood up to her full height. Paused. Then went on. "I, too, want to thank my diplomatic colleague." She continued. "My name is Dr. Devora Ezrahi. I am a medical doctor and the Israeli Ambassador to the U.N. You may have seen me on T.V. I am proud to represent my country. I was referred to Batsheva, that's how I called her, because she was especially talented in dealing with the special dilemmas of diplomats. Children caught between home and postings. Between diplomacy and authenticity. Between being a PK (preacher's kid) and allowing themselves to rebel and find their own way. To confess, at first, I was skeptical. I have a military and medical background and believe in actions. Yet she taught me that words too can be actions. I owe her…an enormous debt. May her memory always be a blessing." There was a very long silence.

The next person to speak called herself Kitty Jambou. She was very distraught and kept saying "I can't believe it! I can't believe! Last night she came to me in a dream. We were together in the park and then we were in the lake together in a rowboat. She suddenly pulled off my wedding ring and threw it into the water. Then she said to me, 'Now, you will always know where it is.' Then I woke up. I immediately looked for my wedding ring. It was still there. What does it mean? I wish I could talk it over with her. She was so good with dreams." She sat down slowly.

The next to last person to speak was an olive skinned man. He said his name was Abdulaziz Al-Sabah, and he was speaking for both himself and his wife, Hikmat. They had also been recommended to Batsheva, that's what she said at their first meeting, "Call me Batsheva. For couple therapy. We, too, are strangers here. From Kuwait, working for UNICEF. We are both pediatricians and care a lot about our work with kids. But the strain of being alone, without our extended family, strangers in a new land, created strains between us, in our family. Dr. Batsheva helped us mend our family and now we feel stronger and more united than when we came. We are going back to our home country next week and today was meant to be our last session. She was… a great lady."

Then it was my turn. I told them how I had knocked hard on the strangely closed door; how it cracked opened; how I walked in her office and saw her, slouching…As I was tearing up, I stumbled, saying, "I tried…I tried to…save her. But it was too late." Refocusing, I broke my silence by asking how Batsheva seemed at their last appointment. And at what time. I desperately wanted to know who the patient was that had seen her last, in the appointment before mine. Most people said that she was as always. Warm, receptive, noble, elegant. A good listener. Each one said there seemed nothing unusual. Only the woman pediatrician from UNICEF, Hikmat, said, she seemed to be writing as they entered, which was unusual. I pushed. "She didn't seem depressed or agitated, did she?"

"No, just as usual. Why are you asking? Don't you think it was a heart attack? That it was something else? What are you thinking?"

Instead of answering, I said, "Since I found …Batsheva"—I almost said the body—"I would be testifying at the inquest tomorrow. I hoped I would see them there."

I wanted to flee; to hide the "great game" I was playing, the evidence I had hidden. But just then the door opened and in came costumed waiters with glasses of sparkling white wine which were handed round to each one of us. The Consul stood up and spoke. He said he understood it was Jewish custom to raise a glass and drink to life, even in such moments of loss. We all stood up, raised our glasses and he said: "*l'chaim!*" We repeated his words. I wanted to smash my glass to honor the dead, like in the movies. I wanted to scream. I wanted to take God Himself to court for all His misdeeds. I wanted to pound on the table, to rip out my hair by the roots, to scar myself, lest I forget. I wanted to rage. I wanted to do many things. But I did none of them. I carefully lowered my glass. Placed it on the cocktail napkin. I nodded to each one. Said "merci" to our host and walked out.

Outside it was a cold but stary night. The rain and lightning had passed. Above me, I could see the stars and their constellations. We make the stars into patterns, the Big Dipper, Andromeda, Leo. But these patterns are in our minds, not in the stars. Each star is on its own.

Chapter 12

Back home, I fell into a dreamless sleep. When I awoke, I was worried I had overslept and missed my appointment with Batsheva. I started rushing to get ready. Only when I started to move my toothbrush inside my mouth, did I realize there was reason to rush, because there was no appointment to go to, because there was no Batsheva—she had been buried in the cold, cold ground.

Grief's like that. At first, you don't believe it; then your mind takes it in, but not your shoulders; when it finally penetrates your shoulders, it has a long way to go before it stabs you in the gut; and trickles across your penis and spills down your legs to stab you in the feet. Once it gets inside you, top to bottom, body through soul, you're never the same; there is no more meadow grass because your existence knows that at any minute there can be an ontological earthquake: a gash opening up to nothingness.

Then I remembered. I did have an appointment. Ironically, just at the time I should be meeting Batsheva. 11 a.m. The inquest. I thought. Did I have to wear a tie? I hate wearing them. Why do we even wear them? They made no sense. Tied, choking you tight around the throat, pointing to your balls. Was this the essence of manhood, of masculinity? Woman didn't have to wear them. They could have dresses, or blouses, sweaters or pant suits. As a woman you had lots of choices, even if it went with lots of personal anxiety. But us white collar guys, we have suits and ties, and nothing else. I wanted to be defiant. To do it my way. To show that the collective could not crush me. But I chickened out. In view of the circumstances, I went with a tie. Black.

The trouble started when they were swearing me in. "Do you swear to tell the truth, the whole truth and nothing but the truth, so help you God?" I had no trouble saying the truth and might even finesse the nothing but the truth, but how was I going to get away with avoiding the whole truth. It was probably a felony to have stolen those papers in the first place. It was certainly going to be perjury if they asked me if I had taken anything else. I recalled what a lawyer friend of mine had advised her clients. I said: "I do."

The questions were mostly focused on establishing the time I had arrived at Batsheva's office; whether I had seen someone entering or leaving; how long it was between when I discovered the body and calling 911. When I said I had attempted to breathe the breath of life, the coroner noted how brave I had been. The autopsy revealed that she had been dead by the time I entered the room, just as the EMT guy said.

Then, suddenly, I was excused. I felt like a schoolboy who just had his most demanding final exam waived. Since it was an inquiry, there was no cross. Cross examination is tricky. There, lawyers are allowed to browbeat you and ask leading questions. Now I was liberated. I sat down and waited for the testimony of the medical examiner. He was a tall Asian-looking guy, with a Brooklyn accent, called Jeremiah Wu.

I know it sounds incongruous but he was probably more American than I was, third or fourth generation Yankee.

In any case, he testified about his credentials: Harvard Med, Fellowship at Yale, former president of the American Academy of Forensic Pathologists, author of over 200 articles and two online textbooks. This guy was good. He knew pathology, histology, anatomy. He testified in a lot of mumbo jumbo that I couldn't really follow. Finally, they asked him the big one. "What in your opinion is the cause of death, Dr. Wu?" He hesitated and looked down. Then, he pulled himself up straight and said: "Dr. Engelman died of an overdose of Batrachotoxin, which is a highly toxic poison derived from tree frogs. We did find a tiny puncture wound in the bend of her left arm. It is most likely that the poison was administered at that point." The questioner went on to the final terminal question.

"Dr Wu, in your opinion were you able to determine whether the death of Dr. Batsheva Engelman was a case of murder, suicide or accidental death." Dr. Wu did not hesitate this time. "Given the currently available evidence, I am unable to make that determination."

"Thank you, doctor."

He stepped down. The court adjourned until a later date when further evidence will be available to determine the nature of the death. I felt my suit pocket burn. I had the evidence they wanted in my inner pocket. But they were never to know what it said. I still wanted to believe that she was killed; and if she did really kill herself, then I really didn't want anyone else to know. I wanted to protect her and her good name. I wanted to be her Galahad. Or was it Lancelot?

Chapter 13

I stepped into the street and started walking. Then it started. Heart pounding. Sweating. Nameless dread. I am going to die. Right here on the street alone like a mad dog. No one will even know my name. They say the worst thing is to not have a name, or have your name forgotten. And, it was happening to me. I was forgetting my own name. I was dying without a name. Then I looked up and saw an ice cream parlour and I realized: that was my trigger. There always was a trigger. Knowing there was a trigger was good. Panic had sense, order. Triggers could be saviors like when Batsheva taught me how to go lucid in the middle of a nightmare by looking at my watch. Seeing the watch made me understand that a nightmare was a dream, a dream I could change. I could say to my mother, I don't want any ice cream and we could walk away. Just walk away. My breathing slowed; my heart beat slower. I felt the ground. I calmed myself. This morning, I said to myself, you were a coward and wore a tie. Now Lancelot (or was it Galahad?), go into that ice cream parlour and order a double helping of pistachio. I opened the frosting frosted door, walked up to the freezing counter, and said it. "Pistachio!"

They were all out.

My next stop was with the forensic hand writing expert. He kept me waiting but finally emerged. "A most interesting specimen. You say you found both items on her desk. Just lying there. Very interesting, yes."

I was waiting for him to say more and finally spoke up:

"What did you find?"

"What did I find? Look at those loops, these slants, the pressure on the 'f,' the movement of the pen on the comma." I waited. Why wasn't he telling me more.

"Yes, there is no doubt, no doubt at all. It's obvious. As clear as day."

"What is clear?" I screamed at him.

"Why," he replied with scientific aplomb. "It is clear as day, with high level of certainty, that in every respect, these two documents were written by two different people."

I gasped.

"Are you certain?" I managed to say.

"Yes, with a high level of certainty. The suicide note and the patient list were written by different people. It's possible someone else wrote the patient list for her and she wrote the suicide note. Do you have another specimen of her handwriting for me to examine?" By nostalgia, I had been keeping her last hand written receipt in the wallet in my pants pocket, like a linking object to her. It was the last real connection with her. I pulled out my wallet and handed it over.

"Oh, yes," he murmured. "This is clarifying. Now things become clear. I can now state firmly that Dr. Engelman did not write the suicide note. It was written by another hand. Probably a woman."

I was reeling. I recalled the dream. Now I was right. She had been murdered by an injection of toxins in her left arm. What should I do? I know I should call the police, that detective what's his name. But then I would have to reveal what I stole and why and that would certainly make me into a suspect. I needed to know the truth. Why was she killed? Who hated her enough to end her life? Maybe she had a patient who was a sociopath? Maybe it was a borderline who lived so close to the edge all the time. Maybe it had nothing to do with her practice: a spurned lover, or a demented neighbor?

The only clue I had so far was the suicide note itself.

I had to find a safe space to look it over, because it was the words of a killer.

Chapter
14

The suicide note lay before me.

As I stared at the lines, I started whispering:

"I knew it wasn't you, Batsheva.

I knew you would never do such a thing to me.

That you would never leave like my mother did."

I started reading:

"I, Dr. Batsheva Engelman, being of sound mind and body have decided that my life is no longer worth living and therefore have decided to end it now. Please do not attempt any efforts to prevent this. My will is in a drawer by my bed at home. To my patients, I say farewell. Perhaps we will meet on the other side."

The note must be full of clues as to the identity of the murderer. If only Sherlock Holmes was here to help me. Suddenly, from within my imagination, the voice of Sherlock began speaking: "Elementary, my dear Fellow! Can you not see how the note was written in haste, in a legalistic style utterly incompatible with an authentic suicide note? Real suicide notes contain instructions to those left behind and feelings of love and regret. Not vagaries like 'I've had enough'. If you consult my little monograph comparing authentic and faked suicide notes, you will discover that this so-called suicide note is entirely fictious. Note, too, her request not to attempt any efforts to prevent death. Individuals who are serious about suicide jump off buildings, so there is no way they can be saved. The will is an interesting touch. I wonder if it is even true. The crass *ave atque vale* to patients is an enormous blunder. A therapist might say, 'I am sorry. I care about you, but I cannot go on like this. Please forgive me.' But worst of all is her misunderstanding of Jewish views of the afterlife. Jews for many centuries had no idea of an afterlife and even when it appeared, it was typically referred to only as *olam haba*, 'the world to come,' with almost no specific discussion of what it is like. Certainly not a place where individuals of all religions and faiths meet up in some sort of an eternal group therapy session. This is flip. Dismissive. Almost certainly written by someone unfamiliar with traditional Jewish theology. If Dr. Engelman had written, at last I will be with my family again, my beloved husband and beautiful children, then I might have had my doubts. Reunion suicides do happen. But this is not reunion, it is insulting kitsch."

Shivers ran through me. I was looking at the hand of a murderer. A woman who would take life with impunity; who had snatched away someone who meant more to me than gold and silver. Who injected her with terrifying toxin and left her for me to find her— otherwise why did it say do not attempt any efforts to prevent this, unless she **knew** I would find her! Unless it was meant for me to find her!

I thought back to the memorial toast at the Consul's house. Was I sitting next to her killer? I wish I had her appointment book to see who had the appointment before me. I wish I knew if her will was where the note said it was. Then the phone rang. It was the police detective. He said there were new developments in the case. He said he needed to speak with me right away. I had to come to see him at the station. I hung up the phone and went stone cold panicky. How could he have found out about the letter, her suicide note? I am someone who avoids confrontation, always. Call it being a goody-goody, call me a wimp who will weasel away from a fight. Call it conflict avoidant. Call it whatever you want. I couldn't stand him shouting at me, calling me a liar, a beggarman, a thief. I understand how people confess to crimes they didn't commit. If he was really angry, shouting, demeaning me, I'd confess to anything; not only to taking the papers but to committing the murder itself. Anything to get him to stop.

I needed a strategy. Then I remember what Linda, my lawyer friend told her clients: "Only answer the questions asked. Never volunteer information! If you start shivering and sweating say, 'Being in an office brings up bad memories.' Don't worry. He's a policeman, not a therapist, he's not going ask you why."

When I arrived at the station, I had to go through more security. Did I say already I hate security? I call it in-security. It's connected to another nightmare which I had a couple of times. In this nightmare, I am at the airport with my Mom. We're going on vacation together and I am really excited. Then we come to the security check. Mom goes through no problem. But when I arrive, an alarm bell goes off; everything freezes. I know they are not going to let me through. I try to call out "Mom!" but nothing comes out. I see my mother walking away. I try to scream but what comes out is a moan and I wake up hearing myself whimpering. Batsheva said it was a dream about painful, even traumatic separation. She must be right. Because on the day she took me for ice cream in the mall, there was a terrorist attack. She was killed and I was not. I was holding the ice cream cone full of pistachio ice cream. In slow motion, I saw her and the ice cream fall down in slow motion. I didn't speak for ten days.

When I arrived at the detective's room, he was very friendly. I pretended to be; to return his greeting warmly, but inside, I was on extra high alert. How could he have found out about the suicide note? It had been in my breast pocket all the time. Was he a pickpocket artist? No, I didn't think so. He was relaxed. He pulled out a cigar and even offered me one.

"I can't smoke. They give me migraines." He nodded in commiseration. "Poor schmuck," he was thinking. "Can't handle real pleasure." But I was thinking why do all these alpha types smoke big, fat, smelly cigars, barbecue at home and cheat on their wives? Is that what is awaiting you at the top? But then, he was all business. "I told you kid there was a break in the case and it concerns you."

Alarm bells went off in my brain; hyper sirens. Beep! Beep! Beep! Whoop! Whoosh! Whoop! I was in panic attack mode.

But he went on like Uncle Ben: "When we got the court order to break into her apartment, we found her will…on the left side of the bed."

I gulped.

He murmured. "Yeah Whadja know?

Anyway, it lists all her possessions, bank accounts, investments, how she wants to be buried next to her next of kin, to donate her books to her Institute and then comes the big surprise. She names you as her Executor."

"What?? There must be some mistake. I was her patient."

""Yeah I gotta confess it was kinda of surprise to us, too. So what I want to know is if you got anything to say about that? Like why did she choose you?"

This news came as a jaw-dropping surprise to me. "I was her patient, not her lawyer. I was never even at her apartment. Never. She was a total mensch. It's a mystery to me. Are you sure she meant me and not somebody with a similar name?"

"Not only is it you, but she has your phone number, your social security number—we checked—it's you all right."

I stumbled on, "I don't know if she had any relatives."

He was way ahead of me, "Well, now that you ask, we did look into that. She had a sister, much older than her who used to work in the foreign office. They are pretty tight lipped in Israel these days, what with all those terrorist attacks. Everything there is on a need-to-know basis. We need to know and they say 'No!' But the sister died three years ago. Anyway, now we must ask your permission to enter into her email accounts, investments and bank accounts, online trolling—whatever might help us with the case."

"With finding her murderer," I added.

"Yup," he said, "that's priority number one."

Chapter
15

"Sign here and here and here and add your initials, here and here and here. Here are the keys to her apartment; and here are the ones to her office. Remember, kid, you are not the inheritor, only the executor. You gotta file reports to the Wills and Testaments Commission quarterly. You can get sample forms from their website. You got a lawyer? No, I didn't think so. Best get a lawyer. Help you round out the edges. What's *kosher*, what's *traif*. Here's a list we provide in cases like that. You can choose at random like in the old days but best to have a look at their record online. I'm with you on murder. But we haven't ruled out suicide yet. Even though we haven't found the suicide note...yet."

I felt nauseous but also relieved. He went on summing up the situation, "No ethical complaints nor law suits. As you said, she was a real *mensch*. Yeah, so the psychological autopsy comes up clean. Suicide is almost out. Which leaves us **with** murder. Murder most foul. You always gotta go back to basics with murder. We know the means. Injecting her with that frog toxin. We're looking into suppliers. Opportunity. Her door was open. Even you found it open. Motive. That's the big question. It could have been a disgruntled patient with a what do you call it, a whopping negative transference; or maybe the husband of some wife she helped see the light of divorce; or maybe it was just a walk-in. Someone who hated her for something unconnected with her practice. Hate's a powerful thing. 'We hate that which we often fear. Stronger than lover's love is lover's hate. Hate is a bottomless cup.'"

I looked at him astonished. He just smiled and explained: "I was a classics major." Gosh! A cop who knew his Euripides. The next thing he'll start spouting Socrates and the Symposium. I always thought cops were down to earth, evidence-based realists, not part of the post-modern antidote. How do you feel when you are not allowed to feel?

The detective went on: "The classics often provide us with a voice for feelings that cannot be put into sound. As Khalil Gibran used to say, 'in happy times, at the base of my soul is a wordless song.' Or Primo Levi, saying 'those who had returned from the camps after seeing the Gorgon, came back wordless.'"

I was…wordless. Why had she made me her executor? It didn't make any sense. I was her patient. She was looking after me, me and my panic attacks, my loser life feelings, my despair beyond despair of never having a mother's hand to hold onto. Now I realized that she was like my mother. Symbolically holding my hand as I took baby steps back into the adult world. For so long I had felt unseen in my bones. Then in that therapy room. She **saw**. She saw **me**. She saw **all** of me, accepted **all of me**, as I was, with all my horrible bits. She even liked me. I know she did, because of the way she smiled. The full Duchenne smile. The one you cannot fake. Maybe she saw something more in me than I saw in myself. A task, a destiny to look after her, after. Maybe she saw I could be a mensch. I could be a mensch for her. Nobody had taught me how to be a mensch. For once in my life, I didn't want to let someone down.

I took the keys and left. Outside, I felt disorientated. I didn't know where to go. I sat down on a bench and started breathing heavily. Please no panic attack now. Pretty please with sugar on top. Focus on your breathing. In…out…in…out. I looked up her home address on google maps. It was the other side of town. I saved the GPS coordinates. I looked up and realized I wanted to have my session. I know she wouldn't be there, but I decided to go anyway. I heard about this crazy therapist who gave his key to his therapy office to one patient while he was away for a few months. She would come to water his plants and sit in the sacred space, like in the serenity of sitting alone in a quiet church. She'd told him it helped her survive the long hours of his absence. Maybe I could sit quietly and restore an anchor into my soul.

I got up and looked for my car. It wasn't there. There was an undignified gap where it had been parked. Was it stolen? Towed? Oh, no! Is this the way people go over the edge? Not from mind-exterminating loss, but from the camel straw of parking tickets. I started my deep breathing again. In…out… in…out. Use the three rules of finding lost objects:
Number 1. Where did you see it last?
Number 2. Where should it be?
Number 3. Where can't it be?
Bang. Number 3 hit me.

It can't be here because I had come by taxi, exactly because of the parking trauma. The car was not there because it had never been there. It was like, *saudade*, a yearning for something you never had.

I went home. The car was back where I left it, where it was supposed to be. I felt the relief of fully receiving back what was irretrievably lost. It is a unique moment when the boundaries of the possible and impossible blur, and life seems possible again.

Chapter 16

I entered Batsheva's office, now not as a patient, but as her executor. I looked at my chair, then hers. I wondered right away where I should sit. I had heard of these trickster patients who defiantly sit in the therapist's chair; or even therapists who don't care which chair they sit in. I felt like a page boy standing in front of the throne of Queen Victoria, daring each other to be the first to put their backsides there.

I wondered what the world looked like from on high. I took a few deep breaths and tried not to think about ice cream.

I shut my eyes and sat down in her throne. When I opened my eyes, I realized she had such a different view of the office than from her patients' chair. Straight in front of her was a Vermeer. I remember seeing it in Amsterdam at the Rijksmuseum and it had made such an impression on me there. It was called, *Woman in Blue Dress*, but in fact it was so much more.

There was a pregnant woman, standing, reading a letter, next to a long table with a number of high-backed chairs. In the background, there was a large map. Strange that I had not noticed it before. Strange, too, that she chose this for her altarpiece of the therapeutic space, her temenos. It must have signified something important about therapy and its process: hearing the unconscious via a voice of a person writing from faraway; and, something new about to be born. But why the map? The chairs? And that special blue, a lapis lazuli, that the catalogue said had come all the way to The Netherlands from Afghanistan.

I also saw that there was an old fashioned clock below the painting so that she could see the time and know when it was time to end. I often wondered about that. As I sat in the chair, I clutched the wooden armrests, as I felt a panic attack coming on. I squeezed them tight and to my astonishment, heard a click. The left armrest moved just so slightly. Was I imagining it? Was I dreaming? I looked at my arm on the armrest and it was indeed shifted. I had a horrible flashback to finding her door open just before I found her dead in this very seat. I shook the thought away. Now, I pushed the armrest deliberately. It slid easily. A marvel of modern carpentry. When I pushed it fully aside, I saw that there was a space, a cavity; and in that hidden drawer, there was something.

It was an exquisitely decorated box with Ukrainian floral designs in red, black and gold. Swirling. I held it in my hand. It was neither light nor heavy. I shook it. It made no sound. Why would Batsheva have a secret compartment in her chair? Maybe she didn't even know about it and it had belonged to the previous owner. It sounded like something out of Sherlock Holmes. I put the box down and wondered what to do. I tried the other armrest but it never budged. I went back to the box. I pushed, tugged, and turned the box, but it never moved. Inside there must be a secret compartment. Compartmentalization is a defence mechanism I knew all about. I had lived my life in compartments. "Little box, against what are you defending?" I tried banging. Using the same pressure technique that had opened the armrest. Nada. Nothing. Zippo.

"What is inside you, my pretty little friend?"

Chapter
17

I looked around the room again. Over to the left, there were long, cream colored curtains. Something impelled me to walk over and pull them aside. There was a small marble shelf hidden inside. And on the shelf, there was something which made me jump. It was a tape recorder. A digital one. Instinctively, I shouted. The recorder began to move. When I stopped, it stopped. When I spoke, it flashed on. Noiselessly. It was, I suddenly realized, a voice activated recording device. Why would she need a voice activated machine in her office? I knew some therapists, especially trainees, recorded sessions to bring to supervision, or for research purposes. Professional ethics always required explicit permission, consent forms, legal documents, signed and certified.

Batsheva never asked me anything like that, and I certainly would not have agreed. Since hacking has enveloped our living space, nothing cyber is safe anymore. Hackers can enter anywhere and the next thing you know your intimacy of intimacies are online. Unless. Unless, she was recording without permission. To improve her technique. Or something more macabre. I quickly thought if she was recording, then perhaps, just perhaps, we might hear her murder. I rewound and pressed play. I listened to the silence with nervous expectation. Who would I hear? The French Consul? The Kuwaiti couple from UNICEF? Maybe my session. I shuddered. Maybe there was a more innocent explanation. Maybe, Batsheva just dictated notes aloud and wrote them up later. Maybe. I listened more attentively. But there was only silence and more silence. The red light flicked on and off to show the thing was working. Silence has many, many voices. I felt I could hear all of them.

If she was murdered, the killer knew about the recordings; maybe she was killed because of them. Killed and then wiped clean. I pressed the rewound button and then play. To my surprise, I heard something on the tape.

It was Batsheva. She was speaking, "You are early." You could hear the door close. Perhaps footsteps on the rug. Then. Abruptly, "No! No!" Then only silence and more silence. After a few moments, the sound of the door shutting. After a longer pause, my own voice, "Dr. Engelman? Batsheva?" I realized that I had been listening to Batsheva's murder and more. I had just missed bumping into her killer. My panic attack started gearing up.

I lay in the chair. Stunned. The killer had sat in this chair and had come into this very room, not to confess but to kill the confessor. The killer seemed like a regular patient; someone who Batsheva knew and expected, only a bit early. He or she, walked through the door; then over toward Batsheva and then deftly seizing the prepared syringe and injecting her in the inner side of her elbow. Then without a sound, walked away. Never uttering a word.

There was no stopping now. I knew I had to find out. Even though it was going to be dangerous. If they killed once, they could easily kill again. I remember some Rabbi from an antique land said how do you feel when you commit a sin for the first time. Bad, yes. And the next time. Less bad, for sure. And the third? The third time you feel great. It's not like a sin, it's like a *mitzva*! Kill and kill again. Victims become like ants. Do you care about the ants when you stroll down the street? No. You just keep walking. But for the ants, it's the holocaust.

The killer had come just before me. They were "early." If I could find out Batsheva's schedule, I could name my suspect. Did she have an appointment book? Or keep her appointments on her phone. I started searching her office for both. I couldn't find either but I came across something that struck my attention. It was a paper that she had given at a Psychotherapy Conference called, *Treating Diplomats and their Families: Persona and its Discontents*. I am not sure why but I stopped my searching and sat down (in her chair) and started reading. It appeared that Batsheva was indeed an expert at treating diplomats and their families, having treated at least seventy-two cases.

There were two interrelated points. First, diplomats needed to keep up a strict persona in their work. The occupational danger was they would continue doing so in their home life. This façade placed enormous burden on their children who were forced to participate in this false self, never saying what you really think, never being naughty, never making a mess. Quite naturally, this was a horrid atmosphere in which to grow up.

The second point was even more intriguing. She claimed diplomats were surrounded by secrecy. In this sense, Batsheva claimed every single diplomat had the psychology of a spy, living a tortuous double life. This secrecy could make therapy problematic since by instincts, diplomatic patients were reluctant to give up their secrets, but with the right clinical posture, it was possible to help them unburden themselves and share their secrets.

This situation of course created a spy-like feeling in the psyche of the therapist, because now the therapist had to hold these secrets of state. Secrets, she concluded, could have a corrosive impact on the person, heightening the gap between persona, the outer face of psyche and the true Self. There was an ongoing, draining fear that one would be discovered, found out. A good secret could bind you to your fellow; bad secrets made one feel cut off, or worse, victim of a psychic infection. You heard so many secrets in this room, Batsheva. What did you do with all those secrets?

Chapter 18

I knew if I could find her appointment book, I would find the name of the killer. It had to be the person who had the appointment before me. The one who came early...early enough to kill. Now I started searching her office in earnest. The entire desktop. Drawers one by one. Even under the carpet. Were there more hidden compartments? Or maybe she used her phone calendar to register his appointments. But strangely, there was no phone to be found. Maybe the police took it. I would have to check. But even if the phone was demolished, thrown into the East River, it might still be synched with her main computer. I would have to check that too. I sat back in the chair. Memories of all the times I had spent in this room splashed back at me. The first time especially....

It was no time for memories. I pulled myself out of the chair. It was like the end of the session. Time to go. I scanned the room once more, the paintings on the wall, the flowers in the vase, the wastepaper basket. I yearned for one more look at her eyes; her smell, her step, the way she opened the door. There would be no more. We bury the body, but not the soul. The soul lingers and does not know it is dead.

I drove to her house. I knew from the police detective that I would have to make a serious inventory of her worldly possession even though it was the unworldly ones that counted for me. I drove into her driveway and parked the car. But couldn't move. I stayed frozen. Not knowing how to move. Not knowing what I would find inside. Maybe it was a bad dream and I could look at my wristwatch soon to remind myself, it was time to go lucid; to tell Batsheva, "I had the craziest dream last night; you wouldn't believe it. I came into your office…" But I knew from my shoulders down through my testicles that this was not a fantasy. It was life, brutish and short.

I don't know how I got out of the car but I found myself at her front door, struggling to get the key into the lock. I pushed it in, but it wouldn't budge. I pulled it out and tried again. Again nothing. Did I have the right key? I double checked. Yes, it was the right key for the correct lock. Yale. Like the University in New Haven, only different. But it wouldn't budge. I looked through the keyhole and saw a darkened room. I even rang the doorbell. Something was off. I had the right key. The right address. The right door. But I was outside. It sounded very symbolic. Holmes reappeared in active imagination: "Elementary my dear Fellow. Someone has changed the lock." Changed the lock so I wouldn't be able to get in? I tried one last time. The key slid in smoothly. But remained fixed in its vertical position. What was in this house that someone did not want me to see?

I was just pondering this when my phone rang. It was the Consul. He said he had heard that I had been appointed Executor and now he wanted me to return his lost object. I knew the Bible made a big deal about returning lost objects. There was a passage in Deuteronomy 22:1 I knew by heart: "If you see your brother's ox (or his sheep) straying lost, do not ignore, it, but surely take it back to your brother." I knew I had a moral obligation to help. But I also knew the Talmud required certain conditions. The owner had to provide proof it was truly his, or hers. So, casually I asked him what it looked like. He answered that it was an exquisitely decorated smallish box with Ukrainian floral designs with red, black and gold swirls.

"It was very precious," he said, "and had been in the family for generations." As he spoke, my soul went cold. I started sweating; my mouth went dry. I couldn't speak. He had just described the box I had found in the secret compartment of Batsheva's chair.

After a too long pause, I blurted out, "Where did you leave it? Where do you think I can find it?"

The Consul laughed. "I placed it into her hand and she said she would keep it in a safe place. I am sure you will find it. I am counting on you. You have my number and my email. Let me know as soon as you can." And he hung up. There was no doubt that the box was his. He had given irrefutable proof. Yet, I had no plans to hand it over. Yet. First, I needed to know what was inside. What was the big secret?

Then it started. Sweating. Panting. Dizziness. Feeling like I was about to die. What if the Consul knew I was holding out on him? What if he kidnaps me and tortures me until I revealed the truth?

What if he sarcastically said, "I knew you are a wimp, not a real man," like my father said over and over again.

Like in an old movie, he would tie me to a chair and say: "Just a little pain and the beans come spilling all out of you. You disgust me!" Then he would tie me up bound foot to hand

and leave me in basement of a derelict building to die a slow, isolated death.

"So long, sucker!" would be the last words I would ever hear. The door would close and I would be left, alone, helpless in the dark.

I caught myself staring down that dark tunnelway. "Breathe." I spoke silently from somewhere inside. "Deeper. Even deeper. Think of Batsheva. Only Batsheva. Imagine her eyes seeing you, seeing her, seeing you. She would not want you to react this way. She would say there is fantasy and there is reality. Sometimes fantasy seems more real, more 'attractive' than reality, because it is more intense, even because it is so painful. But fantasy is fantasy; it tried to protect you from trauma in the past and it mistakenly thinks you need that protection now; but you don't. You are strong. Strong enough to take on reality as it comes."

I heard her words and shook off the darkness of my imagination. He is not going to torture me because he is not going to find out that I already know about his secret box.

Now I understood what it was like to be a spy. Part of me felt so uncomfortable that I allowed him to see me for who I was not. It was false. Worse. Deceit. Yet another part of me really enjoyed it. And not just because I found his box, but because of the secret knowledge that I knew he didn't know who I really was. I had a clean identity behind the persona, untouched by his gaze.

And there, I was safe.

Chapter 19

I wanted to go back to her office and have another look at the box. I drove quick and recklessly to her office and nearly ran a red light and then a stop sign. Maybe Mr. Big was trying to tell me: "Slow down. You're going too fast." But I was too far into my adrenaline high. Someone had killed my therapist and that wasn't business! It was personal! I might forgive someone who wronged me, but I could never forgive someone who hurt someone I love. There, I said it. The "L" word. I was no longer ashamed.

I did **love** Batsheva. And... And.... I felt that... Yes! She loved me, too. Not like a lover, of course. She certainly was not my type; but like a mother. Like a mother who loves her baby to the very core. She is mine and I am hers. For once, I did not feel like a panicky wimp, but a hero on his journey to rescue the Truth from the shadows of perversion. In a way, I felt I was rescuing Batsheva from disgrace, from the shame of suicide.

When I arrived at the office, this time there was no parking at all. I went around three times chanting shamanistic incantations, but found nothing. I know some people pray for parking and today I could see their point. I finally found a spot ridiculously far away. Walking through the light drizzle, I tried not to think that finding a parking spot was directly related to whether you find your place in life. Once you start thinking symbolically, everything is strident with significance and soon, it's elephants all the way down. Maybe this is the way psychotics feel, or people on LSD.

Each branch, each motion imbued with meaning and terror. The universe is waving at you. I entered the building but stopped at her door. Suddenly, I was in a time warp. I was back at that time when I stood in front of this very door wondering whether I should knock again. Not knowing how my life space would be changed for ever. Then it started. Pistachio ice cream. Becoming dizzy. My heart pounding. Cold sweat. Knowing for sure I am going to die right now in front of this door.

Terrified, but too paralyzed to move. Then for no reason, I recalled a story about Joseph from *Midrash Rabba*. When Joseph was in Egypt, serving Potiphar. While he was away, his wife started seducing Joseph. She was beautiful, sexy and she wanted *him*. According to the Rabbinic account, Joseph was fully aroused. He wanted her, he desired her. Just at the very last moment, suddenly, his father's face appeared before him. Then, he knew it was wrong. If he had penetrated, he would never be able to face his father again; he would never be able to face his Master, Potiphar, nor face himself. So, he stopped, did the right thing, and suffered the consequences—a false accusation of rape by the rejected mistress and the prison pit.

I needed Batsheva, now more than ever. I tried to call up her image, those soothing eyes. Nothing. Death was caressing my left shoulder, telling me, "Come." I pressed down harder on the floor. I starting deep breathing. I scrunched my shoulders up toward my ears, tight, tight and then let go, feeling the relaxation ooze into me. Again. Again. And then. She appeared. Rising from the grave into my imagination to comfort me and release me from the panic attack vise. I could see her and was seen. Presence is, was and will be. I relaxed. I unlocked the door.

Chapter 20

This time the room spread out before me like a set table. The chairs, the table, even the pictures were like familiar friends. I said hello to each object and felt a renewed connection. Even without Batsheva, I regained that special sense of being at home in the universe I had felt only here. I realized how my serenity flowed from the sacredness of the space, a magical circle which protected me from my daily anxieties, from my panic attacks.

I sat back down in her chair. I swiveled the armrest and exposed the secret hiding place. There was the Ukrainian box, exquisite, bursting with color and energies. I took it up in my hands. I understood it would not be opened by force but by finesse. I slid my palm beneath the box and gently drew my fingers along its sides. Subtly, it began to move until the top slid perfectly away from the bottom, to reveal the inner sanctum. Looking closely, I saw. Black plastic round things. Microdots! Microdots held in a special container. Microdots are famous from *The Avengers*, *Mission Impossible* and even a recent Margaret Atwood novel. They were first invented by a desperate Frenchman during the 1870 German siege of Paris allowing carrier pigeons to fly them through enemy lines. Microdots are a clever way of conveying ridiculous amounts of information. I could see why the Consul wanted his box full of data back. But wait? Something didn't make sense.

Why would he give a box of microdots to his Batsheva?

I knew therapists were not supposed to accept gifts. It was part of the ten commandments of therapy. Except maybe a goodbye gift. That was kosher. But nothing extravagant. I once heard of a patient who spent the last session listening silently together with her analyst to a favorite piece classical music, Schubert's "Improptus" No. 2 in E flat. Maybe everything that needed to be said, had already been said. Endings are important but complicated. Very tricky. I know I had spent most of my life avoiding them. The death of my mother at the mall would last me for several lifetimes and many rebirths. It was amazing that I was dealing with Batsheva's demise as serenely as I was. Maybe it was because I had a purpose or maybe it would just hit me later, right in the kisser. Kapow!! I needed to think. I needed Sherlock back on duty.

Suddenly, he started speaking again from within me: "It's elementary my dear boy! Either Batsheva received the microdot willingly or under duress. There are only two possibilities. If it was unwillingly, then the murder might have taken place during a struggle; but since the floral box remained in her possession, we can easily discount that possibility. Surely the assailant would have recovered the box at all costs. Therefore, we can conclude she received the floral box willingly. Now that opens up new lines of inquiry. Do therapists usually receive gifts? You yourself have answered that question. Rather, 'Batsheva' was not acting as a therapist, but acting as a spy. She might have been a cutout. A cutout is a mutually trusted intermediary that facilitates the exchange of information among agents, without knowing the identities of the others in the spy ring. From this perspective, Batsheva could easily pass microdots from one patient to another."

We tend to think of Spymasters as males, but the most successful and outstanding of all espionage rings in WWII were led by women, the Spymistress. It seems more likely that Batsheva was the spymistress, the leading espionage agent. Now let us consider motive, means, opportunity. Motive remains obscure for the moment. But clearly means and opportunity were available. A spy-therapist could easily obtain the secrets in one of two ways. The relentless logic of my inner voice went on: "Patients often develop a strong emotional attachment to their therapist. It may include parental-like devotion to the therapist, or even what they experience as 'love.' A spy-therapist could easily manipulate vulnerable and dependent patients for purposes... of espionage. One might specialize in the treatment of diplomats."

I gasped.

"Alternatively, a patient might be encouraged for his own self-enhancement to take up a position which would provide access to sensitive materials. Moreover, we cannot rule out a second, more sinister approach. Again, it is my understanding that patients are specifically encouraged to say everything that is on their mind, to reveal all secrets. Withholding any, even the slightest detail is seen, again by the good doctor, as the violation of the fundamental rule. As a result, the therapist hears the most intimate and embarrassing secrets."

I could not contradict the fundamental rule of free association.

"A ruthless spy would have no scruples at blackmailing her own patients in order to force them to turn over secrets. The methods need not be brutal. Even just the threat of an anonymous letter to an unsuspecting spouse; posting fake news on social media; or even acting as a withholding punishing parent, refusing to have sessions until the secrets are delivered. Therapists, actually are the ideal spies."

I was in despair.

I felt like Batsheva had died a second time. My beloved therapist—a spy!

Could it be true? She was nothing other than attentive, supportive, reassuring, insightful. She never asked me to do anything except shut the door. Even the bill, I always paid before she had time to ask for it. Martin Buber, one of my favorite philosophers, (and not only because his Mom abandoned him at the age of 3!), had this complicated idea. We were not actually individuals. That was an illusion. We were always part of some actual or imagined relationship: an I-Thou, if you were lucky; an I-It if you were not. You were always yourself but also at the same time, being seen, experienced as part of the other's relationship with you. That's surely, the way it is with babies. There are no babies by themselves. Say "baby" and you are already saying "baby and mother." Babies without "mothers" just stop living and die.

Chapter 21

I sometimes think of what my life would have been if Mom had not died. She would have continued telling me stories of Greek mythology at bedtime. Medusa was so cool. I loved how she could turn people to stone with a single glance. Mom would cook my favorite snacks and tuck me in at night. She would shout at me in the morning to get going, or else I would be late for school. I wouldn't have to explain that empty space in my heart at each parents-teachers meeting or graduation ceremony; maybe, just maybe, I wouldn't have married Refrigerating Gretchen if she had been there to hold my heart.

But best of all, I wouldn't have this horrible feeling that somehow it was all my fault. If I had chosen another flavor, say, Chocolate Fudge, then she would be alive today. I know it's not rational, but that's how I feel. Guilty for being alive when she's not. Batsheva told me it was normal to feel such agonizing emotions. Yet, I am forever tormented by the question:

"Why did I survive when she was so much more deserving?"

Sometimes, at night, under the covers, I wish that I had died instead of her; but I know **that** would have been even more terrible for her: to live without me. So instead, I worked out a better solution. In my alternative reality, we would have both died in the blast. Then we would be together. Always.

... I know you're going to ask about the bombers. I will just tell you straight up they were never caught. It's a cold case; a case with a cold. And I know what you're thinking: Catching Batsheva's killer might help me get just a tiny bit of closure.

Maybe.

Maybe you're right.

Chapter 22

I needed a plan.

First, I needed to find somebody who could tell me what was on those microdots and do it in confidence, without alerting the FBI, CIA, MI5, or whoever was in charge of espionage and counter-espionage these days. I knew a sweet, savvy gal who worked in a microfiche library from when I was working on my crappy undergraduate thesis. I felt I could calmly trust her. She would either do it herself or know somebody who could. She would also tell me how much it could cost and how not end up being under the jackhammer of some blackmailer.

I need a "blind job": print but don't peek; just make sure that the resolution is good enough. Then I would have to find somebody who could look at it and make sense of what it was or whether it was in code or *en clair*. I didn't know anyone in the world of spooks or counter-spooks. But I would jump off that bridge when I came to it.

Next, I needed a suspect list. Detecting is a lot like medicine. In medicine, after interviewing the patient and identifying the list of symptoms and signs, the doctor makes a list of D/Ds. To the uninitiated, D/Ds stands for **Differential**

Diagnoses, the list of all the possible diagnoses starting from most likely down to least probable. Then one applies Sherlock Holmes' method. After eliminating what is impossible, what remains must be true. So, too, in murder investigations, one makes a list of suspects. After eliminating each, one by one, eventually, you discover who must be the killer. I let my mind flow and imagined myself as Hercule Poirot sending out invitations to all Batsheva's patients who I had met at the Consul's place. When they had all gathered, I would dramatically turn towards them and say: "You all had the opportunity to kill Batsheva; you all had access to the poison which killed her which can be easily ordered online and finally, you all had motive." The assembled would gasp and shout back incredulities.

"She was my beloved therapist!"

"Why would we want to harm her?"

"You must be mad!"

but I would hush them with "Oui, mes petits! You all had motive because Batsheva was blackmailing you to be part of her spy ring! Blackmailing you with your own secrets that you had so willingly revealed to her. Yes. This is the Truth. Yet, only one of you did it. Perhaps it would be more exciting if you had organized to kill her all together like on the Orient Express, but in fact, neither of you knew of the other until, you met at the funeral and now again in the Consul's office."

One by one, I would say why each was crossed off the list, until only one name remained, Monsieur le Consul Decavalier. Pointing my outstretched finger at him, I would say: "J'accuse! You killed Madame Batsheva. You were very clever, coming early, injecting her, leaving no prints. But you made a serious mistake. You asked me if I had found your Ukrainian gold-black-red floral colored box, an heirloom you said. Your grave error was that you believed me when I said, 'No.' In fact, I had already found it in the secret compartment in Batsheva's chair."

With a flourish, I would pull the box out of my suit pocket and raise it aloft and say, "Here it is!"

The Consul, then, lunges for it. But I hold it up high out of his reach. He then takes out a revolver and says in a rather overdramatic manner, "Give it to me or I'll shoot."

"Oh," I replied rather nonchalantly, "Here, you can have it!" He takes the box with venom. Revenge and desperation united in a single grunt. He skillfully opens the colorful container and stares inside.

He looks at me. Poirot says: "You did not think that I would actually bring your cargo of microdots to our encounter, did you? I am afraid they are as we speak being scrutinized by the appropriate authorities. The game is up, Monsieur Consul. James Fenimore Cooper of the FBI is waiting just outside this door to arrest you."

That's how it would go... in fantasy.

Batsheva always said I had a problem distinguishing fantasy from reality, and she is right. I am not the kind of person who is really cut out for reality. So many scary things are just waiting to happen. I know if I just relax, let my guard down then something truly terrible is going to happen. I knew fantasy would not help here. I needed to buckle down and look reality in the eyeballs. Where to start? I thought back to the memorial meeting at the Consul's. The people there should be on my D/D of suspects. I had made a note of who was there on my cell phone after the meeting. Let me see if I could find it.

Yes, here it is: under suspects. The number one, prime suspect was the Consul himself, Mr. Decavalier. He was a foreign service professional who is paid to guard secrets. He also wanted that beautiful box, full of microdots. He is number one.

Then there was that high powered executive John Cohan. His name sounded Irish, but it could be Jewish, a variant among French Jews for Cohen. I bet he travelled a lot. Maybe he was the courier. Maybe the Mastermind. I'll bet he had a lot of secrets he would be ready to kill for.

Then, there was the Silent Lady, who was too choked up to talk. I would need to find out more about her. I could try calling again as a bereavement counsellor. It sounded like she really needed help.

Another stronger contender had to be Dvora Ezrahi, the Israeli Ambassador to the U.N. She said she had a military **and** medical background. Her posture was ramrod and up straight. I bet she knew how to kill and walk away … easily. She was tough. But she seemed genuinely grateful to Batsheva. Yet as a diplomat and an Israeli, she must have lots of secrets to hide. Israelis certainly have a reputation for taking people out dramatically. Like assassinating the Munich Olympics Murderers, one by one. So, strong on method and opportunity but a big question mark concerning motive… I'll leave her at number four.

Then there was Kitty Jambou, who had that strange dream in which Batsheva told her to throw her wedding ring into the pond, so she'd always know where it was. It reminded me of some movie from long ago. She was a big unknown. Her name sounded French. Maybe she was also an international.

Finally, we have to consider the UNICEF pediatricians, Abdulaziz and Hikmat Al-Sabah. If you went by popular

Islamaphobic prejudice and spy fiction, they would certainly be the guilty ones. Batsheva was Jewish; they were Moslems. Is there anything more to say? Like in Latin America, if a man and a woman are alone in a room for more than 33 seconds, no one will believe they did not have sex. I agree it's painful to realize that's how people think today. People are no longer individuals but only representations of their collective identity.

But gosh! There are pediatricians after all…and at UNICEF. How more goody-goody can you get? And yet, who knows what evil lies behind noble facades, in the scar tissue of the heart. Consider Harold Shipman. He was a sweet and beloved family doctor in the Midlands, until someone realized that there was a surprising high number of people dying in his practice. Eventually he was outed as the most prolific serial killer in history, killing over two hundred fifty of his patients. Can you ever really know? Can you?

I am sure Batsheva had other patients who didn't come to the memorial; and of course, it didn't have to be a patient, although the recording certainly suggested it was. Maybe it was the plumber who came early. Or the cleaning person? Certainly, someone who knew how to give shots. I wouldn't know how to use a syringe. So that leaves me out. Now that could be a very useful clue. Who had a medical background? Or was a diabetic? Or a heroin addict? Someone who knew the difference between a vein and an artery. Someone who could shoot straight. Someone ready to send you to heaven or Kingdom Come. Someone who could. Someone who would. Someone who did!

Chapter
23

The next day came up grey. I wanted to stay in bed, to pull the pillow covers over my self. But I knew I had to get up and face the computer. I had set myself the task of searching all of my available names to see if there were letters after their name, like M.D. or R.N. or had trained as a phlebotomist. Or else was arrested on narcotics or had a history of diabetes.

It would be easy to see if anyone had medical letters to their name. Maybe it was someone who dropped out of med school and turned to diplomacy instead. Running down narcotics charges was in the public record, but it was only by jurisdiction. To be ultra-sure, I would have to search fifty states, ten provinces, their country of origin and even then, I wouldn't be sure. Medical records were another thing altogether. They are severely confidential, hacker-protected, or supposed to be. I heard of this black hacker team that stole mental health data on thousands of Finns and got enormous amounts of ransomware. And they aren't the only ones. Medical blackmail is a growing, high profit industry. Unless a suspect went on the record as a diabetic (and why would they), I would never know.

I faced the computer. My blank screen.

Then it hit me. Abdulaziz and Hikmat! The pediatricians from Kuwait. They surely knew how to inject. Although they said they came to Batsheva for couples work, one could have come alone. That's the way couple therapy works. The therapist listens to both sides separately, and then figures out how to put them back together again. Like Humpty Dumpty. In individual therapy, such talking behind your back is forbidden. I certainly wouldn't want Batsheva to hear my ex's venomous version of me.

I didn't know much about UNICEF and almost nothing about Kuwait. My computer informed me that UNICEF was indeed the oldest organization supporting the rights of the child in 190 countries and territories, providing vaccinations, sanitation, help for poverty, child abuse and child prostitution—they took it all on. And in the worst places to be a child: El Salvador, Mexico, Pakistan and these were countries **not** at war. They really did good. As for Kuwait, all I knew about it was oil-wealthy, Saddam Hussein and not much else. I would google it later. Strange, how we know a name and yet nothing about those people. Suddenly, my fellow mourners, these Kuwaiti doctors, bounced from the bottom of my suspects' list, right up to the top.

Uncharacteristically, I decided to ring them right away. I found their number and called. The phone rang, then rang and rang. And rang some more. I knew he was not going to answer. But then, suddenly, I heard Abdulaziz speaking: "Farewell New York, Hikmat and I have returned to our homeland, Kuwait. We can be reached at our new international number or at our usual email. Please do not leave a message. Salaam Aleiku."

Only when the answering machine went "Beep," did I understand that they were gone and the voice was only a recording. Yes! Now I did remember. At the memorial at the French Consul's, they said they were returning home. Returning home is not always a picnic. Ask Odysseus.

I felt stumped, stymied and stuck.

Chapter 24

If Batsheva was a spy, I had to understand her place in that realm of shadows. I heard there was a new spy museum downtown that included memoirs by real agents in a "spy and tell" exhibit. I gazed through the index of reportage and my eye caught on an entry: Recruiting. It was by a Kazakh Intelligence Officer who ran double agents in Iran, for the Soviets. Here is what he said:

"There are four ways to recruit an agent. Love, ideology, money and blackmail. Love is the best, since people will do anything for love…even betray their country.

Ideology is good… as long as it lasts. But even if the agent goes shaky, you can usually effectively blackmail them with the evidence of their own deceit. Money is the worst. A money-spy has no moral or emotional constraints. They can you sell out at any time: either to a higher bidder or worse, decide that they had enough and get out of the game, permanently but with all their secrets dangling. Blackmail is the most reliable. Fear of shaming is something hard wired into the psyche and its intensity goes back to a wordless place of terror of what we fear most: exclusion, ex-communication, solitary confinement."

He went on:

"Blackmail works so well because each of us lives a double life. There is something each of us feels we must hide, whether insignificant or essential. We are all symbolically spies, living a double life. Therefore, intelligence services always prefer to recruit with blackmail. And the dirtier the better. Because then, you always know where you stand. Fear is the key. Fear and terror."

Then I had a most terrorizing thought. What if Batsheva had tried to recruit me?

I imagined her as combination of Mata Hari and my Mom looking deeply into my eyes and saying, "You'll do it, won't you? You'll do it for me?"

Then I would melt into a pool of agreement. I wouldn't say anything but only shake my head up and down. The idea of saying "No, you manipulative bitch!" (which I said to Gretchen often) would never occur to me. It would feel impossible; a betrayal of all that is good and true and shining in bright lights. After I microfilmed that first file, there would be no going back. I would be her spy and her slave. "Speak Spy-Mistress: I will obey."

What about Ideology? Personally, I am an "end of ideology" kind of guy. Intellectually, I understand how ideology can give people so much meaning, belonging and togetherness. But look at the price! Ideologies kill people, just for being who they are: Jews, gypsies, class enemies. I think I feel immune to an ideology gambit.

And yet, in another hyperreal fantasy, I could imagine Batsheva inviting me for Shabbat dinner. After lighting Shabbat Candles, she would say: "Please call me, Sheba! All my close friends do." ("Is she saying we are close friends?!")

Then, in the flickering light of chicken soup and candles, she would say: "You know, my mother was in the Camps. Not Auschwitz, but Belsec. Worse. If there is an algebra of suffering, much worse. She remained alive. Alive, but a *galmuda*, alone and abandoned. Without father, mother, sister, brother, aunt, uncle…She knew what it feels like to wake up in the morning where there are men, and women too, whose greatest Joy is create a world without Jews."

I didn't know what to say. No one had spoken to me like this.

She continued, "So, yes, I am a child of a survivor. A second generation. I grew up in the shadow of those I will never meet… as a memorial candle. My life is not my own. My mantra is: 'Never Again!' Never again will Jewish people face annihilation of God's hidden face. Today. Even today, Jews face that threat. There are many nations who wish for a Jewless world. Not just Arab nations, who surround us. No, many others, too. The idea of exterminating the Jews originated in France. The English exiled Jews more brutally than the Spanish. In fact, in the entire world, there is only a single country that never practiced antisemitism.

"Do you know what it is?

"No? Then I will tell you: Georgia.

"And there is only one country which saved 100 percent of its Jews during the holocaust.

"No, it is not Denmark.

"Unexpectedly, it is a Moslem country…

"Can you guess?

"Yes, Albania!

"Today, the threat is not gas chambers but nuclear war. You will say it is a threat against all of humanity. And it is. Surely. But nuclear weapons will be used against us, first. Why? Because we are Jews. That's why. I have seen your hidden gifts, your striving for security because you, too, are a survivor. Now I will give you your survivor mission. It can be your life work and something more. It can be your contribution to 'Never Again.'"

In this fantasy script, I would be overwhelmed. I never actually met a survivor face to face before. She would have entered my imagination so acutely that I would agree to do whatever she asked.

Then, I thought of her name: Batsheva. For me, "Batsheva" has a warm, soft, soothing sound. The first syllable, "bat" coming up fast before slipping into the smooth of "sheva." It had a stop and flow rhythm of gentleness sounding together. Then somewhere in my collective unconscious, I recalled that Batsheva was a name coming from the Bible. I searched until it popped up in Second Samuel and what I found was shocking. Batsheva **was** Mistress of Deception and Magician of Manipulation.

Beautiful Batsheva made sure David, the King, saw her sunbathing nude on the rooftop of her Jerusalem penthouse. David desired her. Invited her. Made love to her. Impregnated her. Even though Batsheva was married to one of David's own, mighty men, Uriah. To cover up their sin, the King ordered Uriah back home from the front lines, to spend a creative night with his wife. But being the honorable soldier he was, he refused. He would not, could not, go to his beautiful wife while his men were on the battle edge. Stymied by such devotion, and to disguise the adultery, the King sent Uriah back to the front carrying a secret directive to his commander in chief. In that message, David described in deliberate detail how to arrange Uriah's death on the battlefield. Here was the plan: Uriah's unit was to march into battle. At the critical moment, his men were secretly pre-ordered to withdraw, leaving Uriah exposed to enemy fire.

"Where is the best place to hide a body?"

"On a battlefield!"

And so it was.

As a result, the newly widowed Batsheva became Queen, then Queen Mother. Later, she easily manipulated the Old Man into making Solomon, her own "replacement" child, king. From Desire to Empire in just a few chapters of Scripture. If my Batsheva was anything like her Biblical namesake, I wouldn't stand a chance.

After I left, I experienced a strange sense of loss, a yearning for a normal family, a simple, everyday happiness that I had never known. Having Batsheva's box felt like a special secret. It filled some of the hole that could never be filled. I remembered a college friend from happier times. Her name was Laura. She had come to see me after visiting her best friend, Caroline. Her friend was in the hospice, dying, in the city where they grew up. Dying very soon, maybe even that very day. Laura and Caroline had wept and hugged, hugged and wept. Then, Laura, my friend, got up to leave, when Caroline called her back saying, "Just don't buy a Golden Retriever! OK, Laura. No golden retrievers!"

I didn't understand. So, Laura explained. Back home, where they had grown up together, the "perfect family" had a husband, wife, two children and a golden retriever. My friend was saying remember me and my two children who will never ever have a perfect family, never.

And Laura started to cry. Her friend was not yet dead, but Laura was already mourning her... and she would never stop.

Chapter 25

Then I remembered something vaguely from a psych course I took back in college. It was something called, *Zeigarnik Effect* named after, the famous *Bluma Zeigarnik*, a Soviet era psychologist, student of the great Kurt Lewin. She discovered that unfinished tasks are remembered much better than completed one. The urban legend said she had gotten this idea while talking to a waiter in his restaurant. The waiter could remember all the details of every order, until it was served and paid up. Then he would forget. It was as if there was an inner monitor keeping the orders vivid in the mind. But once the bill was paid, the details were deleted, to allow mental space for the next order. This was how I felt about Batsheva's murder. It was mentally unfinished. I needed to know who had killed her and why: only then could I begin the process of forgetting.

If I never found out, the memory would haunt me. I realised this must be how the fear of ghosts began. The ghost is a disembodied expression of the incomplete, unresolved relationship between the living and the dead, who are not resting in peace but coming back to haunt us.

I appealed to the man in the deerstalker hat to return one more time... Then, after an agonizing delay, Sherlock Holmes appeared vividly in full dress from the edge of my inner world. In my mind's video screen, he arose with his pipe, deerstalker hat and all, saying: "Elementary, my dear boy! The key to solving the murder lies not in opportunity, nor the means. But in motive. Once we understand the motive, the prize is ours. As you may recall from my little monograph on the subject, the motives for murder are seven: gain, concealment, revenge, jealousy, hate, thrill-seeing and love. As you can see, the seven motives fall into two clusters: rational reasons and irrational urges. Thus 'concealment' (hiding a crime by burying the body) or 'gain' (murdering a divorcing husband before he can change the will) are rational. Gain and concealment often go waltzing together. These 'rational murders' are perhaps evil in its clearest form.

The other five motives derive not from evil, but from passion and its discontents, from disorders of bonding. The human psyche connects deeply with these damning deeds of love gone very wrong. As your Professor Jung put it, 'It is not whether we have complexes, it is whether they have us.' Looking at the conditions of the murder itself, we can quickly eliminate gain or concealment. Thrill seeking seems particularly improbable. Patients who do kill their healers tend to be disgruntled psychotics, not free-wheeling psychopaths. So, we are left with the Big 4: revenge, jealousy, hate, and 'love'. I say 'love' with 'quotation marks', because murderous love in typically one-sided: 'I love you passionately, but you don't care about me or my feelings. If I won't have you, then nobody will.' Such unreciprocated 'love', easily slides into all too common, jealousy-hate-revenge axis. Following this line of thought, we might say with a certain degree of confidence that these motives run together."

My inner detective paused and then went on with dramatic flair:

"What is the opposite of love?"

I didn't know what to say. The opposite of love? Does love have an opposite? I thought true love was full, without any ying and yang, incomparably whole. So, I said, "I am not sure. What is the opposite of love? Hate? Indifference?"

That clear, confident voice from within snapped back at me, "The true contrast to love is neither indifference not hate, but rather power. The urge to control the object, we are terrified to lose."

This hit me like a boomerang. I suddenly understood my whole relation with Gretchen in a flash. I had tried to please her, but she didn't want that. She wanted something else and tried relentlessly to make me become the person she loved, who unfortunately was not me. I resisted her attempts to mold me. But only passively; the only way I could win was by losing. For both of us, power was yearning for love. And in that game of love, we both lost. Heavily.

My inner Sherlock was only hitting his stride. His grey eyes were twinkling into overdrive. I was afraid he had gone back to his cocaine. "If we add to the mixture, the element of espionage, then new narrative possibilities appear."

I had almost forgotten the secret compartment, the box and the phone calls from the Consul in my ruminations on Gretchen. "Narrative possibilities?" I echoed.

"Yes, indeed!" But he said no more. I was waiting for the revelation. It felt was as though the line went dead.

"Tell me!" I screamed toward myself.

But Sherlock remained silent. His fingertips touching to form a symbolic triangle. He was Smiling! Even smirking!

"Tell me!"

But he remained wordless. Yet, I felt him looking at me intently.

Then, I had an eery moment. It was like therapy with Batsheva. I would ask, no! demand answers and she would sit there quietly, looking back at me, saying without words, that she would not reply, because...

Because, I knew the answer. If only I would stop looking to others for the answers, I could find them inside me. This was the message: relax and reflect. You will find your way, if only you will start walking. I, Batsheva, am behind you, making sure you do not fall. But now there was no one there behind me and I started crying again.

I gathered my strength behind my tears. I looked at my eidetic image of Holmes, straight in the face and said, "If it's espionage, then we can rule out love, jealousy, or even hate. Then what remains is revenge. Revenge through and through. An impulsive act of vengeance, because Batsheva's killer knew it would be discovered, wanted it to be discovered. Wanted the whole world to know, perhaps as a message to others, to see what happens when..."

But that was the rub. It was not clear at all, what Batsheva had done. Who had she Double Crossed?

Finally, Holmes came to my rescue. "If you follow my methods, it becomes clear that Batsheva was given the floral box by the Consul to give to the Persian. That much is clear. But if, as we believe, she was a Spy Mistress working for another power, then something went amiss. Batsheva likely refused to hand over the microdots to her handler. A Double Cross becomes highly likely. I believe Batsheva's handler became enraged at her defiance and murdered her out of spite. This line of reasonings suggests, as you have believed all along, that the murderer was one of her most important patients."

Yes, this is what I had believed all along. But who?

"Who? you ask? Indeed, who?" that strangely clear internal Sherlock Holmes spoke and then stopped. After a pregnant pause, he continued, "But it will be wiser to await the results of the microdot analysis. But for now, patience."

And he disappeared back into the unconscious and I was left alone, but intensely with myself.

I realized I knew very little about Batsheva herself. I googled her full name. I discovered she was a graduate of Columbia University with a Ph.D. in Clinical Psychology.

Her dissertation topic was on special psychological problems of diplomats and their children—a qualitative study based on interviews with 45 diplomats. She had done advanced training in Israel at Hadassah University Hospital in Jerusalem. She had trained at the New York Center for Analytical Psychology, where she was still a member and training analyst. Analytical psychology I discovered is a cover word for "Jungian." So that's why she was so interested in dreams and "the journey." But then in her personal background came the kicker. She had married a fellow psychoanalyst and had two twin girls, identical, Miriam and Jessica. Everything seemed fine until one weekend, her husband was taking the twins on a hiking trip. She was at a conference in Washington. On the road back home, her husband and the twins were killed instantly by a swerving semi-trailer—I learned all this from a link to their obituary. They waited until the end of her keynote address to pull her aside and tell her the news that destroyed her narrative, forever.

Oh, Batsheva! I never knew.

I never suspected how bereft you were.

I know I wasn't supposed to know
but now I feel so guilty talking endlessly about my pathetic
problems when you had so much...

There were no words to express what happened to you. I
think about you giving your paper at the conference unaware
that the world as you knew it no longer exists; that as you
walk toward the exit, there is the pit, waiting for you to fall in
and scream, silently, forever.

Did you have a brother? A sister? To comfort you, like Job.
Bat Sheva, the daughter of the seven, the daughter of the oath,
you are...
a healer wounded indeed.

How much time did you take off?
Maybe it was easier focusing on the pain of others than to
stay home in emptied rooms.
What made you carry on?
What was His purpose in the grand scheme of things to do
this to you?
If God exists, I want Him punished.

Chapter
26

The Microdots. I make a mental notation to call Sandy, my librarian friend, to see if she found someone who could process them. Then I felt exhausted and fell asleep, even without brushing my teeth. The next thing I knew I was at the airport security check again. My mom had passed through and I could see they were not going to let me. This is where the repeating dream usually ended. My Mom and I separated by the security barrier. But this time, I screamed and the sound of my voice came through, "**Mom! Mom! Come back!**" Mom heard, stopped and looked back from beyond the barrier. Then, she threw me a kiss and said, "You will be fine without me." Then she turned and continued walking. I screamed again, "**No!**" But she was gone. I woke up sobbing. I knew she was…

Gone for good.

Chapter
27

I woke up the next morning refreshed. I opened the window, wide. I took a deep breath. I recalled that there was something I had to do today. Then the phone rang. When I picked up the phone, I heard a familiar voice, to which I said, "Sandy!" She told me that she had gotten the microdots developed and since it seemed so technical, she asked a friend in Applied Physics Dept. to look at them right away. The professor had just texted her and said that there was some mighty interestin' stuff there. I was to call her right away. Her name was Professor Matov.

I called her number. She said, "Come right now, as I have classes later." I grabbed the keys and I went. For once, I felt I was doing what I was supposed to do. Applied Physics was a concrete hive, housed in ultra modern glass. Professor Matov's office was on the top floor, close to the heavens. After searching down corridors, I finally found her door. But I could not move. Another door, flashed before me. Then, I felt like I was falling into a space with no end. I took a very deep breath and an another. Then I told myself, "I am in front of an entirely different door." My inner dialogue continued: "And if microdots contain what I hope they do, then I will become the hero with a thousand faces." I raised my fist, but before I could have courage to knock, the door opened. A slim, energetic redhead came out and without missing a beat said, "Ah, I thought it was you. Common' in! Call me Simcha."

A moment later we were huddled around her desk looking down at the enlarged microdots. To me, they looked like some bizarre x-ray art. But Prof. Matov drew her finger round the images, and said they were clearly centrifuges. "Centrifuges?" I understood how the sound of the later part of the word echoed a Bach fugue or that weird psychiatric condition. I guess I had heard the word, *centrifuge*, but didn't really know what it was. Simcha said that it all started with a pair of brothers who wanted to separate cream from milk. Eventually, they discovered that spinning milk fast enough will cause it to separate heavier cream from lighter lowfat milk. She explained that the principle of spinning is the same whether it is used for blood tests, research, or as part of an industrial processes. In fact, anything that you want to separate sediments from liquids.

She paused and I knew it was going to get serious. Like when Batsheva paused before she gave an interpretation heading like a cluster bomb to my guts. Simcha continued: "But this is not just any centrifuge. This is a special centrifuge, called a Zippe-type centrifuge. A Zippe-type centrifuge has a hollow, cylindrical rotor filled with gaseous compound. A rotating magnetic field spins so quickly so the lighter gas collects near the center, where scoops collect it."

I didn't really understand what she was saying but I knew I had to ask, "What is it used for?"

Her answer hit me directly between the eyes.

Chapter 28

She looked up. Then down. Then straight at my eyes.

"How much do you know about Uranium?" she said.

"Uranium? Not much." I said.

She switched into Power Point mode.

"Uranium!" she said, "U for short, is a silvery-white metal with the highest atomic weight in nature. The most common form of Uranium on earth is the isotope U238. Isotopes have different numbers of neutrons and protons and this gives them special characteristics, like radioactivity. U238 is radioactive but only very slightly. The Romans used it to color glass. In contrast, the isotope U235, is very, very rare but is so radioactive it can trigger a nuclear chain reaction. If you slow down the chain reaction, you can get clean nuclear power. If you enrich U235, you can make nuclear weapons."

Immediately, I understood. The French Consul had been passing nuclear secrets to the Iranian, Jafari. I wondered what was the Consul getting in return? Cash? Embargoed oil? Blackmail?

Yet, I knew that neither of them could be Batsheva's killer, because they each desired that Ukrainian floral box. But if not them, who?

Chapter
29

I thought for a moment.

There was only one country that would use all extreme measures to stop Iran from acquiring nuclear weapons.

And it was Israel.

The Israelis had made numerous attempts to sabotage the Iranian Nuclear Program, from stealing their nuclear archives, to assassinations of key scientists, to the devastation of missile complex and power plants. But the most dramatic and effective had targeted the all-important centrifuges, so essential to making nuclear devices. Natanz in province of Shiraz is the most important plant for uranium enrichment in all of the Islamic Republic, with 20,000 gas centrifuges.

It is the key production plant in the Iranian plan to create nuclear weapons. In June and July 2020, nine separate explosions struck Iran. The most decisive and destructive was at Natanz, where three quarters of the centrifuge facility was destroyed. It set back the Iranian nuclear weapons program for years.

To me, there was no question that the Israeli Mossad had recruited Batsheva, perhaps even in the schmaltzy way I imagined she might recruit me. Or when she was working at Hadassah Hospital, researching the life of diplomats. Batsheva had only one Israeli patient who could possibly fit the role of her handler: Dvora Ezrahi, Israeli Ambassador to the U.N. She was a doctor, diplomat, fighter. Who says she was not also a Spyess? Batsheva's handler and "pretend patient." I checked Ezrahi online. In her medical background, I discovered she was a specialist in toxicology – that would explain that frog toxin. A new news item came up, saying that on the day of the murder, she had been recalled to Israel for urgent consultations. She was out of the country and likely never coming back. She was beyond confrontation, beyond immunity. I wondered what Batsheva had done that caused her to go into such a rage and kill. Almost certainly, Batsheva had refused to give Ezrahi the microdots. Maybe Batsheva didn't like the new Israeli policy of targeted killings and bombings. Maybe she didn't like being bullied and blackmailed. Maybe she felt it was time to stand up and say "No!" I would never know for sure. But at least, now I knew the how and the why so I could begin to forget, to mourn, to let go.

Chapter
30

I gathered the microdots from Simcha and put them back into the floral box. The box seemed lighter and so did I. I looked at it closely and asked, "Where do you want to go?" I knew I couldn't give it back to the Consul. That would be dangerous. It didn't seem right to place it back inside Batsheva's chair. Nor alert the FBI. I didn't want it in my apartment.

I asked the box again, "Where do you want to go?"

Then I knew.

I walked down to the riverside. I found an old landing. Carefully, I placed the box in the water where the current would carry it. I watched it slowly make its way toward the ocean. Until it disappeared.